Chronicles of Ériu Series.

ISBN: 978-0-9956214-4-2

Published by Waring Estate Publication.
Email   publication@waringestate.com.
         Info@chroniclesoferiu.co.uk

Printed: Waring Estate Publications.

THE CHRONICLES OF ÉRIU.

VOLUME 4.

THE FOMORIANS.

BY

MICHAEL H ST.C HARNETT

ILLUSTRATED BY KASEY LEITCH

Lebor Gabála Érenn

Ireland - whatever is asked of me
I know pleasantly,
Every taking that took her
From the beginning of the tuneful world.

.

A long life fell
to my lot, I shall not conceal it;
till Faith overtook me
from the King of Heaven of clouds.

.

I am Fintan the white
Son of Bochna, I shall not conceal it:
after the flood here
I am a noble great sage.

Section III, Book XXI Verses 1, 11 & 12.

This book is dedicated to

The Brehons and Bards of ancient Ireland who, for many millennia, dedicated their lives to the memory of the Irish experience so that we may understand it today.

It is my great wish that their dedication is now recognised and appreciated as their interpretation of our shared history, rather than as just a fanciful rendering of myths and legends.

Glossary.

Affreidg – Cessair's birth land, now flooded by the Black Sea.

Ancients – Those spirits, gods, and people of prehistory.

Angus – leader of the axe-making tribe on Rathlin Island.

Antonio – Santorinian sea trader

Api – Mother Nature

Balor – Leader of the Fomorians

Banba – Cessair's 'right hand' woman and later a tribe leader.

Bards – Ireland's chroniclers and storytellers.

Bairrfhind (Baa-fend) a Brehon, becomes Bith's young wife.

Bith – Cessair's father.

Bóinne – Boyne River settlement area of great holy importance.

Brehons – The interpreters and administrators of the law.

Bridget – A powerful female druid (a spiritual leader)

Cailtach – Female Druid High Priestess, a spiritual leader.

Capacirunt – Scythian master builder's settlement in Egypt.

Cessair – The leader of the first tribes in Ériu.

Cethlenn – Balor's wife and Kallisti's daughter.

Curragh – A small boat made of branches and animal hides.

Dot – Balor's father.

Dublin – The black pool.

Dún na mBárc – The fortress of the boats.

Druid – Spiritual leaders

Elgnat – Partholon's wife.

Ériu – The 'Land of Plenty' now called Ireland.

Ethniu – Balor & Cethlenn's daughter, Kallisti's granddaughter.

Feinius – Father of Nel & Nenual, a leader of many Scythian tribes.

Fintan – Inventor and Cessair's husband

FirBolg – Literally 'The Bag Men' – men who moved soil & rock.

FirGaileoin – Literally 'The Spear Men' They dug the ground.

Fomorians – Those who came from under the sea.

Giza – Egyptian Holy centre and future site of the Pyramids

Hatti – Leader of the Hittites

Hippolyte – Amazonian warrior leader from Azzi.

Hittites – Scythians who settled in Anatolia (now Turkey.)

Kallisti – Sardinian trader and former explorer.

Ladra – Cessair's childhood friend, Sea captain & shipbuilder.

Li – The river Bann

Manandan – Ériu's God of the sea

Merkhet - Instrument of knowing or pendulum

Meroe – Cessair's home in Egypt.

Nel – brother of Nenual, a friend of Cessair.

Nenual - brother of Nel, interpreter to the Pharoah.

Nubia – Then the southern part of Egypt.

Nuralgi – Tall lookout and signalling tower, first seen in Sardinia.

Pyramid– π, *Ra* (Sun God), *Mind.* The link between man and God.

Partholon – Scythian tribe leader and businessman

Ra – The Egyptian Sun God.

Saball – Egypt's Pharaoh, Cessair's foster father.

Santorini – Mediterranean island proficient in making copper,

Saqqara – Early Egyptian Holy centre

Scotia – Cessair's Goddaughter and Saball's granddaughter.

Scythian – The people who lived in Affreidg before the flood.

Sera – Partholon's father, leader of one of Affreidg's largest tribes.

Sherden – Sardinian Sea traders.

Sí an Bhrú – Newgrange, the Boyne holy settlement.

Tabiti – Scythian main god.

Thrace – A country, the Northern part became Greece.

Troy – A city, named after Cessair's horse.

Contents.

BALOR

In Love and War, Changes are Afoot.

"I have such exciting news."

Said Banba as she ran down the gangplank to meet Cessair.

"Our whole world is changing everywhere! I have so much to tell you."

Cessair was surprised that her usually calm close aide had changed into this excited and ebullient missionary. Typically Banba was the quiet, slightly reticent, but also a very hard-working prop that held together Cessair's original tribe and effectively 'ran' Waterford. Something had to have happened, and one look at Banba's face and its cheerful glow spoke volumes; Cessair gave a little smile at her suspicions. Cessair knew that she would hear all about the real reason for her excitement in good time, but first, she had to hear the news from abroad.

"Let's find somewhere to sit and talk, and then we can exchange news."

Said Cessair. Banba's newfound exuberance had caught Cessair slightly off guard, and a chance to relax quietly and talk seemed the right course of action. But Banba, on the other hand, had so much to talk about and show Cessair that calm communication would be very unlikely.

"Come on board and look at the fantastic gifts from Scotia. They can't wait on board a minute longer."

With those words, Banba was already pushing back up the gangplank against the flow of Cailtach's astrologers. They had been summoned from Saqqara and were glad to be

1

back on dry land. They were apprehensive at being brought to such a wild and alien place. Cessair waited and watched as they wearily streamed off in a single file. Bridget and her welcoming party of Druids were waiting there, at Dún na mBárc, to meet and greet them and to whisk them away to shelter and a warm meal amongst the dense woods not far away.

Bridget knew that they needed rest and a chance to be at the top of their game for when, in a few days, they were to reach Sí an Bhrú. Cailtach would expect their best work to commence immediately. It was only fitting, for the great god Dagda, that the edifice they were going to build should be of the highest quality so that they might commune with him.

Banba appeared almost impatient as she waited for Cessair to climb the gangplank and join her. And just as Cessair reached the deck of the boat, Banba was again away, this time across the deck at a trot. She stopped at a wooden barricade, turned, looked back at Cessair and then said,

"Aren't they magnificent!"

It had been a long time since Cessair had been at a loss for words. The sight of those magnificent animals, now gifted to her by her foster child, refused to allow her to compose her thoughts and speak. The only thing to come from Cessair's face was a flood of tears, and a deep aching in her heart accompanied them.

In Love and War, Changes are Afoot.

Just as had happened with the Hazel stick, which had jumped in her hands when she passed over underground water, her body reacted to something beyond her control. Cessair was ordinarily cool, calm, and collected. She needed to be, to be the great leader she had become, but the sight of those magnificent horses instantly reminded her of all the best happy times of her life long before she came to Ériu.

She had not realised how much she had missed her horses before. She thought of Troy, her first real horse, that she had as a young girl; everyone had said how he was far too much of a handful for a little girl – but he wasn't. She had bonded with him immediately, and they shared so much of her youth.

It was Troy that took her on her first big adventure to look for the snow in the high mountains, the adventure in which she encountered the long-toothed tiger. It was Troy that carried both her and her best friend Dana when Dana was poisoned and close to death. It was Troy that shared her fun and secrets for all those years before Affreidg was lost to the flood. Troy was with her when she, with Hippolyte's help, first led her tribe out of Affreidg and when she thwarted Balor and saved the Hittites from capture and slavery. It was Troy who helped her to find the site of the great town that she named after him.

She thought of Scotia, granddaughter of Saball the Pharoah. She thought of the little girl who had never been out of her private palace until she was almost ten. The little girl she had taken from that palace to Meroe as her foster child and pretended to the world that she was her daughter. Scotia, the girl who had never ridden before but once in Meroe, mastered the basics in a few days. Scotia learned to ride and to love to ride. She thought about that little girl, her 'daughter,' that shared her life with her for more than five years before Ériu. Scotia loved riding so much that almost every day they would, at least partly, be spent on horseback; even at the formal Pharoah's functions, they would usually arrive on horseback.

She thought of the last time she, Scotia and Nel saw her friend Hippolyte and her Amazonian warriors in their best finery. They had been lined up on their horses in salute, flanking the gorge out of Azzi.

From the first day she met, Scotia knew how to pull Cessair's heartstrings; this time, she had surpassed herself. There right in front of her, behind the barricade that Banba was gleefully pointing at, stood a fine young stallion and three young mares and two of those with colt foals at foot. Cessair knew just by looking at them that they were from Troy's bloodline, and the tears gushed even more vigorously.

Banba was expecting some reaction from Cessair but nothing quite so emotional. She knew Cessair was passionate – she had to achieve what she had – but it was always under control, always in check. Banba was secretly glad that there was no one else close by to witness this scene; she felt it would not stand well with Cessair's persona of a strong leader.

Cessair remembered the last time she had cried so uncontrollably. It was when she had left Scotia in Giza, and then at that time, she had wept on a place where she felt safe; she wept on Fintan's broad chest. It happened as they started to sail out of Egypt and out of her 'daughter's' life.

Then, she realised that these horses reminded her of her life before Ériu when Cessair could be a girl, a woman, almost a mother. Now she was just a leader and had to play that role all the time, and she had to sacrifice everything else to be that person. Yes, she had married Fintan, and maybe they would have children, but for now, their focus was on her people and Ériu.

She had never mourned the loss of Affreidg, nor had she mourned her carefree childhood cut short by her grandfather. He had placed the hopes of their fated nation on her incredibly young shoulders. But now, in an outpouring of emotion that lamented all of her losses, feelings were raised from deep within her, and they came flooding back to her consciousness. For the first time, these repressed feelings expressed themselves physically as tears.

She realised that all these beautiful, sad, and happy memories made her the person she was today. She also realised that she was happy with whom she was now.

Now that she understood the cause of her repressed tears, the aching she had always felt was at last acknowledged. The hurt was lifted as it was carried away along with those long-stifled tears; that pain would be soon gone forever!

5

Cessair now, for the first time, understood why her grandfather Noe, despite being Ardfear the leader of all Affreidg, had no compunction to hide his true feelings. He, too, on occasion, would weep openly. She realised, that last day when she left him, that she was weak when she turned and left her grandfather rather than show him her genuine emotions. She was weak when she couldn't show or accept her emotions when she left her foster father and 'her' precious Scotia; again, she had been weak even though at the time she told herself, *'She was being strong for Scotia.'*

Cessair was now sure of herself; she was a strong woman, a leader and those tears were a vital, integral part of her. She now had no need, or desire, to suppress or hide them anymore.

The arrival of Antonio and Banba's reaction to him confirmed all of Cessair's earlier suspicions. One look at Antonio confirmed that his feelings for Banba were mutual. As he approached them, he said,

"We need to unload these horses quickly; they have been on board for a long time. Scotia insisted that I look after these animals and gave them the easiest and safest passage of all my passengers, even beyond the care of the astrologers! She told me, in no uncertain terms, that if anything should happen to these horses, I should not return to Egypt! At the same time, she gave me enough money to enhance the rental fee to purchase this ship outright in your name."

Cessair was moved, the tears had passed, and she marvelled at Scotia's extravagant gifts. The resource

In Love and War, Changes are Afoot.

required to transport six horses from Egypt would have transported half a tribe. On the positive side, Antonio's ship was an extra one, and there was still space after all the astrologers had boarded. Cessair just said,

"That's my Scotia. She is becoming quite the strong little leader. Banba, come with me and tell me all about her, her life now, and please, tell me about Nel.

Antonio, please join us when you have finished and when you can safely leave the boat and my precious horses."

With those words, Cessair and Banba headed for Cessair's home in Waterford and prepared themselves for a long evening of catching up.

There were several important objectives for Banba's trip to Egypt with Antonio. Still, for Cessair, the news she wanted to hear was about Scotia, and until Antonio arrived, that would be the only topic on the table.

Cessair learnt that Saball's health had deteriorated badly and that he was now a sick old man on the brink of death. Scotia was secretly visiting and helping him. She was now afraid that her father would find her and punish her. As Saball had predicted, he had become power crazy and was already trying to wrest royal control, even while his father, the Pharoah, still lived.

The island state of Meroe was Scotia's lifeline; for a while, she was safe. Even at her young age, she now had a significant following throughout Nubia. Most of that support came because the Nubian section of Egypt loved Saball. They did not like the Pharoah's son's warlike actions, so they chose and trusted Scotia to help them.

Banba quietened her voice to a whisper to tell Cessair a great secret. A secret that Cessair would be only the fifth person in the world to know.

"Saball is allowing and arranging for Scotia to marry Nel!

He worries about his son using her as a bargaining tool in a diplomatic marriage. Scotia was showing great faith in me that she told me, but she took the chance because she wanted you to know; she loves you so much. I swear this secret will never pass my lips again to anyone."

Banba's voice raised again as she continued.

"You know, when I was with Scotia, it was like being with a younger version of you! You changed that girl's life so much for the better."

"Well! What about your great news? Don't be shy. Tell me."

Said Cessair to change the subject in case the tears returned. Banba continued with a great grin on her face and the traces of a happy tear in her eye.

"Is it that obvious? Yes! I do love him. There is no use in trying to hide it. I think I always have since that first day in Santorini.

Remember back then, when I thought he hardly noticed me, we sneaked out of the tent to leave him and Ladra to let them talk about boats. He told me he was upset that I had left that night because he wanted to spend it with me. But he

8

In Love and War, Changes are Afoot.

made up for it when we visited the hot bubbling rock the next day."

"Too much information!"

Said Cessair just as Antonio arrived through the door and joined them at the dining table. He sat at the vacant place set for him; it was set next to Banba's seat. Then he spoke.

"Your horses are happily eating grass in a field. They are grazing by my ship, which is now safely moored in Dún na mBárc. The astrologers have been safely delivered to the hospitality of the rest of the Druids, and now I can sit at this fine table piled with fine foods. I am now sitting close to a great woman I love."

"I hope that you are referring to me!"

Said Cessair, and they all laughed.

Banba and Antonio then gave Cessair a detailed description of their trip to Egypt. The winds and the sea were favourable for most of their way down. The fleet stopped with Kallisti in Sardinia for supplies. He was excited when he heard about the developments in Ériu, and he wished you, Cessair, well. He repeated his warning about the sea pirates, especially now as many valuables were being found in Ériu and that trade was bound to increase. He said that trade around the Mediterranean had dramatically increased and that he saw as many boats in a month as he would have seen in a year. He explained how Hatti had settled Scythian tribes all over many local islands and the northern coast of the

9

Mediterranean and how each new settlement was becoming a trading mecca. His business was booming, and raw material such as the rock that Antonio was carrying was in great demand and becoming extremely valuable.

The next leg of the journey to Santorini was a little slower as there was little wind. Cessair could see the twinkle in their eyes when they spoke about Santorini. Antonio was in full flight, and Cessair knew she would hear every little detail.

"It was great to see home again and meet my friends and family. They were all positively falling over themselves to buy the metal ore we were carrying. Traders from all around the Mediterranean want our island's copper products. Our craftsmen are working flat out, and we still cannot supply what is demanded of them by new trading ships arriving daily. Our craftsmen no longer must take our products to find markets for them; the Phoenician traders and others are all coming to Santorini.

Our fleet of ships is lying idle, so they were delighted to hire one of them to allow us to collect the astrologers from Egypt. The metal ore was quickly unloaded, and the fleet we arrived in went on to Troy without us."

Banba, who up until now had been quiet, continued the story.

"It took a few days to prepare the ship for Egypt, so there was plenty of time to see around the island. I met Antonio's family and friends, and he showed me the sights.

In Love and War, Changes are Afoot.

We even went back to see the hot bubbling rock again but were disappointed that it had stopped bubbling and was cooling down. Everyone on the island was apprehensive about the hot rock no longer bubbling, and they say that the last time that happened, they had terrible problems when it started again. It was so long ago, however, that no one knew what actually did happen or what the god did to them then."

Cessair could see that Antonio worried about what might happen when that rock started to bubble again. She smiled, however, at the thought of the two revisiting their old haunt of the bubbling rock.

She heard that the Santorinians were so happy with Fintan's ore that they let Antonio hire their best boat in the hope that they might do more deals with Cessair and Ériu for much more ore.

The ship they hired was nothing like as large as one of the ships of Ladra's fleet, but she was elegant, swift, and highly manoeuvrable. Cessair heard that the new ship gave them a quick and easy passage to Egypt without real problems. Banba then said.

"We went straight up the great river to Meroe to see Scotia. I thought it best to talk to her first before we followed Cailtach's instructions and took away Egypt's best astrologers. We arrived at Meroe, her impressive island, and tied up against the pier.

A large force of armed warriors immediately stopped us, and they wanted to know our business. I approached their leader on my own so as not to be seen as aggressive, but even alone and unarmed. They still would not let me pass to see Scotia.

I asked them to send a message to her, but even that seemed not to work. Their mood changed when I mentioned your name, and they became my best friends. I still did not pass, but the word of my arrival as your envoy was rushed up to the palace.

While I was waiting and casually chatting, I mentioned Hippolyte, and honestly, you would think that I personally knew a god. They all wanted to hear everything about her, and all of the warriors crowded around me, even the problematic leader. They all asked so many questions about her. They even asked if the famous story about Hippolyte and the camel was true. When I confirmed it was, they all fell about laughing."

Cessair laughed at the thought of the soldiers all laughing at the celebration of Hippolyte's comeuppance. The memory triggered many happy memories with her foster daughter and her friends in Meroe. In her mind's eye, she saw Hippolyte, the fearless warrior, confident that she could master and ride all horses, the leader of her army, galloping into the desert on a bad-tempered camel with no respect for any mere horsewoman. The posse of horse riders vainly trying to catch the errant camel and its powerless rider just made the whole scene even more comical.

A few moments later, her attention returned to Banba's words.

In Love and War, Changes are Afoot.

"It was then when Scotia came rushing down to greet me. She dismissed the guard and sent my boat crew to some building for refreshments, accommodation, and rest. Then she invited Antonio and me up to the palace. There, she had Antonio entertained while she took me aside and asked me all about you and Ériu. I am sure it was a good hour before she even asked me about my mission.

I explained Bridget's find at Sí an Bhrú and how Cailtach had rushed over to see Dagda's haunt. I said that Cailtach was so excited that she just had to have her best astrologers with her. Then, I said you tasked me to come here and collect them, and I was to bring Saball's and her your gifts and news.

We spoke for hours until she told me that Antonio and I would be her guests and stay in her palace for a few days. She wanted to meet Antonio, so she laid before us a great feast that lasted for hours, yet we did not see the time go by."

Cessair learnt that Scotia had already matured into the role of leader and that everyone very well respected her. Everyone in Nubia knew who really brought up Scotia, and everyone there secretly thanked Cessair for it. Cessair was almost embarrassed by those words, but she was pleased that Scotia was respected in Nubia and the rest of Egypt. She smiled slightly when she heard that Scotia was professional enough to treat Banba's envoy work as strictly business and kept it private, even from Antonio.

Cessair was saddened to hear that Saball the Pharoah, Scotia's grandfather and Cessair's foster father, was gravely ill and that, in his public absence, his son was seizing control of Egypt. How her father was trying to undo all of Saball's good governance and replace it with his despotic power. Charioteers had already been dispatched by him to well beyond the regular borders of Egypt. They were sent to claim new territories in his name and for his glory. Things were not looking good for Egypt's future, at least for the average hard-working person in Egypt.

Scotia explained that her father's new war interests should keep him busy for the next few years and that it was doubtful that the removal of Egypt's best astrologers would even be noticed, for a while at least.

She arranged for Banba to meet Nel in Giza and that he would escort Ériu's envoy to Saqqara and act as a translator and intermediary. To many in Egypt, Scotia's patronage was

In Love and War, Changes are Afoot.

now as powerful as Saball's; Scotia could not have helped any more.

Banba's meeting with Nel also surprised her with how much he had changed. She explained to Cessair.

"He is no longer the little boy who needs to be guided about where he may go in Troy. He has grown into a wise young man and a robust and influential member of his tribe. Nenual frequently took his brother to meet with the Pharoah, and of course, Nel could meet Scotia in secret once there. Associating with the Pharoah certainly helped with Nel's social standing back home.

Feinius, the two brothers' father, had just brought with him many additional tribes from Babylon. They came to help with the construction boom that was happening in Egypt. There was now a sizeable Scythian contingent of craftsmen living in Capacirunt. Feinius now controls Capacirunt as an exiled nation within Egypt. They are living on the lands that were given to them by Saball's brother when he was Pharoah many years earlier.

I am so glad that Scotia had Nel help us to meet with the astrologers in Saqqara. If reaching Scotia had been burdensome, meeting the astrologers was much worse.

The city was hot, and it was vast. It was so old that no one could say when it was founded or even who started to live there. It was slow to change, and strangers were not welcome or accepted. It has always been the burial place of anyone significant in Egypt, and the place was more dead than alive.

When it came time for me to meet with the astrologers, no one senior enough to introduce me to them would even consider talking with me, not alone introducing me to them. I was rejected several times at the front of the astrologers' temple gates, and those lowly individuals who stopped me could not believe I knew who Cailtach was. They did not believe she sent me – what an arrogant group of people!

As astrologers, they should have known that I was coming!"

Banba laughed at her little joke and continued.

"Nel was brilliant and clever.

He said to those gatekeepers that there was a significant problem with the instructions and plans for the new pyramid that his tribe was building in Giza and that, if they were to avoid angering the god Ra, then a senior astrologer would need to alter the plans and also be senior enough to sign the new plan off. That got us through the front gate, but some other petty official tried to fob Nel off by saying they would get back to him soon! But Nel was ready for them and said that he would return to Giza immediately and that all work would stop on the great new pyramid so that they would not incur the wrath of Ra for knowingly building the Sun God's pyramid from a flawed design. He added that the Pharoah would not be happy that his building work should stop because an astrologer would

In Love and War, Changes are Afoot.

not quickly fix the critical measurements. Nel then turned on his heels and walked off, back out through the entrance gates and out of the complex. The rest of us stood stunned, and then we sheepishly followed him.

A good half hour later, as we were considering what we should do next, a very red-faced official-looking person hurriedly approached us and pleaded with us to return with him to the central astrologers' temple.

Once inside, Nel would not speak with anyone about the 'pyramid problem,' with anyone other than Cailtach's most senior assistant, and then preferably the one who had signed off the original pyramid plan.

Once, we were all seated in front of an annoyed, blank-faced, but senior official of sufficient rank. Nel then introduced me as being sent from Ériu as an official envoy and emissary of Cailtach, their boss.

The rest was easy, and excitement was visible on their formally featureless faces. I doubt if that bureaucratic lot had even left Saqqara, not alone Egypt; they are in for big surprises in Ériu! I am sure they have never even seen a forest like the one they are sleeping in tonight."

Antonio added that they all enjoyed the spectacle of those lifetime bureaucratic hermits preparing to cross the world in his boat. For the first time in a long time, they were taken out of their comfortable, privileged lifestyle and were being made to join Cailtach at the end of their world. A few were excited and eagerly looking forward to their new experiences and what they might discover about Dagda.

It was extremely late when Cessair heard the last of the story of their mission to Egypt. The journey back was uneventful, and except for the extra stop in Santorini to pay for ownership of the boat with the money that Scotia had given them, it went flawlessly to plan. They had returned to Ériu in record time. Their new boat was not only comfortable, but it was extremely fast.

A few days later, Banba and Antonio finished their special envoy mission when they took the refreshed and now not so stayed astrologers on the short boat trip to Sí an Bhrú.

Cailtach only gave the most cursory of thanks to Banba as she quickly took her experts away to work on a great new design for what they would build for the mighty god of time, Dagda.

Cailtach's behaviour was not rudeness in Banba's eyes, for she had learnt that great visionaries, such as Cailtach, could not see what was directly in front of them in the material world and that they, instead, clearly focused their attention on another realm.

Bith Settles and the Bulls Roam

(Then the Bulls Settle and Bith Roams.)

Cattle had always been a part of Scythian life in Affreidg, but they had no more or less importance than sheep or fowl and certainly not as important as horses. When Cessair met Hatti, she found that the people venerated the cow, especially the bull, as a creature apart. In every one of his tribe's homes was a great set of bull's horns built into one of the walls; in some ways, these horns could be considered a small shrine within that home. They venerated the bull's power and wanted that symbol to reflect the strength of their tribe and people. They even went as far as to wear a small set of horns on their heads when they went

19

into battle in the hope that they might take strength from them and, at the same time, strike fear into the hearts of their enemies.

The presentation of Hatti's small herd of cattle when they left Troy was a grand gesture and symbol of his esteem for Bith. On the other hand, Bith could not have seen the cows far enough; they would not stay around the village where they were meant to be. They were forever breaking out and would test and break the best-made fences. On more than one occasion, they broke into Bith's precious cropping fields and caused much damage. One person could easily manage goats or sheep alone, but these cows, especially the bulls, always seemed to need at least three or four people to regain control. On the positive side, they liked the grass in Ériu, and the herd started to thrive and do very well.

Bith found that a few tribe members had a good way with those headstrong animals, so their lives soon revolved around taking care of them, and in turn, the animals learnt to trust and follow their keepers. The most considerable risk was from a wolf attack. Still, these became rarer and rarer as there was often easier prey for the wolves to feast upon elsewhere, especially when the humans were around to shoot arrows at them.

However, one advantage of big animals grazing in the woods was that they cleared much of the dense undergrowth and made areas of the woodland more accessible. Where areas of the forest were already thin with grass patches growing, the cattle kept small trees and shrubs from invading that area. If fire burnt an area of woodland, the cattle ensured that the only new vegetation that could grow was grass, as everything else did not survive the constant grazing.

Bith Settles the Bulls Roam.

Another advantage of all the vegetation these large animals consumed was that most of it passed through the cows and produced large amounts of rich and very fertile manure. One of the less pleasant jobs for those poor herdsmen was to gather some of this manure for Bith's best crops. In time Bith started to like his cattle and what they did for him.

The crops Bith had planted in the Spring were now ready for harvesting. They had grown well, but they were still too precious to eat! Except for the weakest and smallest seed, every pickle would be needed to produce many new plants in the coming year. Bith had a team of gatherers with nimble fingers and great patience to search out each mature and dry plant and pull up the straw along with their attached precious seeds. They gathered the straws into bundles and then brought them undercover into one of the buildings.

Another group took armfuls of the seed-laden straw from the building and thrashed the seed heads against a large flat rock. The seed and the chaff came away from the straw. Then the people put the straw back under cover. If a wind blew, the mixture of seed and chaff was tossed into the air, and the chaff blew away, while the cleaned seed just fell back down. The cleaned seed was then ready for storing until planting next spring. There was a great crop, but even so, only a little could be used for bread as Bith was hoping to plant ten times the area of crops the next year compared to the area he had just harvested.

Wild creatures, from grubs to quite large mammals, would have attacked and eaten those precious seeds. Accordingly, pots had to be made to store the valuable seed. These pots of seeds would then be shared between all of the tribes throughout Ériu. When in years to come and every tribe was harvesting their crops, they would repay their debt in kind. They might return grain, animals, or even something they had made. The general principle was that they were all one people, even if they were broken up into different tribes, and their primary duty or care was to any person who needed help, no matter what tribe they belonged to or where they lived.

Cessair had arranged to visit with her father and find out how he was progressing with the harvest. She first tried to find him near the grain store, where several people thrashed the seed-laden straw. She asked a busy and very dusty woman.

"Do you know where Bith is?"

"Sorry, no idea, but ask Bairrfhind. She always knows where he is. She is inside counting the filled pots of seed."

Came the words from behind a cloud of chaff. Cessair thought about the words that she had just heard. She even posed the question in her head as she entered the grain store.

"Why does Bairrfhind always know where Bith is? I hardly knew where he was on a day-to-day basis when we lived in Meroe; it was a small island, and he was my father. I must be missing something here!"

As she entered the store, she almost bumped into Bairrfhind, who was on her way out. Bairrfhind spoke first.

"Oh, Cessair! I thought that you were Bith. I was expecting him and was coming out to greet him."

Cessair was surprised by those words, but the idea that popped into existence only a few minutes before had germinated and had its first bud. She thought she would feed that bud by giving it a chance to grow. She said.

"Nice to see you, Bairrfhind. You are a long way from home."

Not even a question, but the bud grew and became a sprout, as Bairrfhind became slightly flustered and said that she was helping Bith with the harvest. Bith already had plenty of people working with the crop, and Bairrfhind, a Brehon leader, would not usually be asked to help with the menial jobs. The kernel of the idea had germinated and had now firmly taken root in Cessair's mind.

Someone approached carrying a large bundle held together by two outstretched arms and interlocking hands. His voice revealed Bith's identity from behind the straw that hid him.

"These seeds are from the best plants. We must thrash these separately and store them in our safest pots."

Before Cessair could even speak, Bairrfhind was over helping and sharing Bith's load. One look at her father's face after Bairrfhind's intervention caused Cessair's idea to bloom.

It positively blossomed when Bairrfhind said.

"Bith, you must be thirsty and hungry. I have prepared food and drink in your house. Come, your daughter is an essential guest, and Cessair must join us - please - there is plenty."

Bith had lived alone for years, and anyone entering his house would have sensed that it was a widower's home, but Cessair now noticed a feminine touch. Nothing dramatic, but little tell-tale signs, such as tidy storage areas, clean plates, and fresh flowers. She wondered how long it would be before she heard the whole story. As it turned out, it was not exceptionally long at all.

Bairrfhind had not just prepared a meal; she had prepared a feast, which was already neatly laid out on the table. Cessair felt almost ambushed but in a friendly way. She knew that something big was coming, and she thought that she had a good idea of what it was.

She was well off the mark, but she had guessed one part correctly. Halfway through the meal, when their thirst was slaked and their hunger diminished, Bith said.

"I listened closely to what you told us about the freshwater sea that you went to last month. I miss our lakeshore life in Affreidg; I was used to it. The river here is ok, but it is not the same. I ..."

Bith paused for a second to compose his thoughts and then continued.

"... We ... would like to establish a new tribe on the shores of that great sea. We would travel up through Ériu, following the coast at first, always heading towards the north, and then we should find that great freshwater sea that you told us about. We will pass through Wexford and Bóinne and mark a new land route. We will learn about Ériu as we travel and find a route on land that can connect our settlements without using Ladra's ships."

"We?" Repeated Cessair, apparently missing the essential points of Bith's statement. It was the smile on her face that told Bith otherwise. She knew that this adventure,

this journey, was the living, experiencing part of life that acted as one of those stepping stones she had learnt about while still a child. The 'we' meant a shared experience, which was what life was truly all about. The journey was the now; the destination was the dream, ambition, and hope.

Bith also realised that he could not skirt around the issue any further, so he said.

"Bairrfhind and I have grown close, and we complement each other very well; she completes me. We want to get married!"

There it was said. Cessair felt a tinge of jealousy as she would no longer be the most crucial girl in her father's life.

But that selfish emotion was quickly replaced by the comfort of knowing that her father would have a new companion to share his life journeys and adventures. Her response was genuine and heartfelt.

"That is great news – I am so pleased for both of you. Tell me more about your plans?"

Bith looked visibly relieved; it was difficult to tell his daughter that he was going to remarry and, what is more, to marry a girl the same age as she was. Now with her approval and support, he looked at Bairrfhind, smiled, and then started to explain the detail of their plans.

They would take a group of people to form a new tribe. Then they would travel first to Ladra's settlement of Wexford. That part should be easy, as that overland route had been marked and is already frequently travelled. They would then head up to the Bóinne settlement and spend the winter there. The following spring, they would head up to find the freshwater sea. They asked if Ladra's ships could bring their winter supplies and spring seeds up to Bóinne for them as they would be heavy for them to carry overland.

New tribes arriving from Troy were expected any day now; for one of them to have a ready-made settlement would be helpful for them. The area that Bith and Bairrfhind were leaving was close to a copper ore deposit, and therefore a tribe with plenty of firbolg should be chosen to settle there. The built houses and food already stored for winter would allow the new settlers to immediately start collecting ore for Fintan, who could smelt it during the winter.

When Cessair returned to Waterford, a tired-looking Banba met her. All the ships returning from Troy had just arrived en masse, giving her a massive problem. She was trying to find temporary accommodation for so many people. She was delighted when Cessair told her to send a whole tribe to Bith as he would relocate them. She was initially surprised, but when Cessair explained what had been discussed and agreed with her father, Banba said.

"One of the tribes that have just arrived was specialising in just that, and they had heard about the ore that we had found here, and they want to start gathering it immediately. They are mostly firbolg and firgaileoin. We must send that tribe to Bith tomorrow so they can settle in quickly while Bith is still there."

Not long afterwards, there was a massive celebration for Bairrfhind's and Bith's wedding. Everyone from a large area participated and used the occasion to enjoy a great party. Cessair was by now a well-seasoned leader, and she was well used to the many demands made of her as the leader, but having her father officially ask her for her permission to marry Bairrfhind, ranked in Cessair's mind as one of the most bizarre. After that awkward moment, Cessair thought.

"Most people marry and settle down; only my father would marry and then roam!"

A few days later, she watched as her father, his new bride, and the rest of their tribe crossed the river and headed north to Wexford. They had started on the first part of their long journey north. She quietly whispered.

"May Tabiti guide you and preserve you."

Cessair looked again at the river a few days later, standing next to a tearful Banba.

There was still time for another trip back to Troy and to return before winter set in properly, and the seas became too wild for travel. Ladra went with them this time as he wanted to talk about trade with Partholon in Troy. Antonio also went as Fintan had gathered more ore. It had been decided to send this load to Santorini again, as there was a good and ready market for an immediate sale.

Cessair wanted to cheer up Banba, so she asked.

"Will you be marrying Antonio when he comes back?"

"We plan to at the end of the year when he returns."

Was Banba's reply. Then a long pause. Then more tears.

"If ... he survives and returns."

"Love can be a harsh companion."

Thought Cessair as she silently tried to comfort Banba with a hug. Then she said.

"Come, let us visit Bridget. She will tell us what is in his future."

Then the two headed off to the woods to find their druid friend.

Black Sails and a Black Shadow Descends.

The whole fleet sailing together gave security if case anyone ran into difficulty. But so many ships travelling together was a logistical nightmare regarding docking at ports. So once the captains knew the route and coastline, they tended to travel in much smaller groups, often as few as two or three ships. Even then, the line of ships could stretch out and become miles apart, but they always knew that the last ships were behind them and following the same route if they should need help.

Ladra was glad to be travelling back down into the Mediterranean. The seas were so much calmer and warmer. His ship carried the minimum crew necessary so that he could bring back more passengers to Ériu on his return trip. His competitive streak made him always want to be the first to reach his destination. He and Antonio started to race each other to see who would be the first to dock at each next port.

Ladra's ship was much larger with a long waterline and carried larger sails, so it should have been faster, but it was wide, heavy, and cumbersome. Antonio's Santorinian boat was much smaller and lighter but long. The length of the waterline dictates the speed that a ship is best suited to travel; despite their size differences, both boats were well-matched for a race.

The larger sail area of Ladra's boat should have still given him a significant advantage, but Antonio's boat's better manoeuvrability matched that advantage. Antonio could more easily turn his boat always to catch the wind at the best angle, thereby more than compensating for his smaller sails.

The two boats were evenly matched all the way from Ériu, with each crew believing that they would win the next leg. As their competition grew more intense, they pushed harder and harder, leaving the bulk of the fleet behind them. As they passed through the Pillars of Hercules, Ladra was well ahead. The bigger ship was better in the big Atlantic waves. But both knew that Antonio's craft should be slightly quicker in the calmer waters and winds of the Mediterranean. And sure enough, over the next agonising few hours, Antonio's ship closed the gap on Ladra's and passed him. They had passed several new settlements on the mainland, but as they both wanted to race on to Sardinia, they did not stop to visit them. A few hours later, Antonio was well ahead but still within sight.

The sun was now bright and warm, and the waters were calm; brisk tailing winds made perfect sailing conditions. Ladra was thinking of ways to catch Antonio. Was there a faster route that he could take? Where were the winds stronger, closer to the coast or further out? These questions were racing through his mind when he saw a flash from Antonio's boat. Then again – there was trouble ahead, and Antonio needed his help as quickly as possible. Ladra could not travel any faster, but he alerted his small crew to be ready for anything as he raced towards Antonio. Now Ladra travelled with a different kind of urgency.

Ladra was sailing as fast as his ship would travel, but he still could not reach or catch Antonio. Ladra's mind was racing.

"Why is he not slowing down? Why did he send me a distress call and still not stop? This distress call is far too serious; he cannot be playing games; what could be the matter?

The two boats were about an hour apart and at the limit of their vision of each other. Several more times, Antonio sent distress flashes – something important had happened. It would be about another hour before Ladra could see the problem close by. Ladra was questioning himself.

"There is another flash; is that another ship with Antonio's? Is that smoke?

Smoke at sea was usually a terrible sign. Wooden ships with pitched decks would burn very quickly, and smoke meant only one thing – fire! The next hour went agonisingly slowly as Ladra approached the two boats, and the reality of what had happened became known. The smoke had stopped about half an hour earlier, so the fire had been put out.

Ladra docked his ship against Antonio's, which was now sandwiched between the two boats. Ladra spoke first as he boarded Antonio's with his pressing questions.

"What happened here? Were those sails on fire? Was anyone hurt or killed?

It was the stricken ship's captain who answered. Ladra did not know the man, but he did recognise his language and manner as Hittite. On the deck, he was sitting next to Antonio; both men were blackened by soot.

"We have just been attacked and robbed. While none of my crew was killed, some have been hurt. Our ship would have been burnt if it had not been for Antonio, and we all might have died."

The man visibly shook as he slowly told what had happened to him and his ship.

"We had brought people to a new settlement in Iberia and were returning home. On our return journey, we collected goods as tributes from other settlements we had set up over the last few years. We carried olives and other valuables and made fast progress across the sea.

I saw three black ships with black sails well ahead and in line with our route. I had heard of these pirates, so I avoided them. They also changed course to intercept mine, so I changed course again to make the best use of the wind. Then they finally caught up with my ship. They were huge and fast. I tried to zig-zag so they could not board me, as we were all moving quickly. They threatened to force me to stop, but I ignored them and continued going as fast as possible.

Then the pirates did something I had never even heard of before, but it quickly disabled my ship. They sailed alongside, but beyond arrow distance, they kept position, so the sun was always behind my boat when viewed from their boats. Then many of the crews, on all three black ships, picked up large pieces of reflective material."

The captain then pointed at Antonio's signalling plate that he had used to send Ladra the distress message.

"They were like those, only much, much larger –as big as to hide a man behind them. They all used these mirrors to shine the reflected sun onto my sail at the top near the mast. The sides of all three boats were lined with a wall of mirrors, all pointing at the same point of my sail.

Black Sails and a Black Shadow Descends

We could not see the men holding the sheets, but we could see their eyes. Holes had been cut out so the men could see where they were pointing their mirrors. With so many mirrors directed at the same spot, it was not long before my sail caught fire. My ship stopped moving, and we all had to try to extinguish the fire. Then they boarded us and overwhelmed my small crew.

He paused while drinking the water he was given and then resumed his story of what had happened to them.

"We were surrounded, outnumbered, and huddled together on the deck while the sail continued to burn above us. It was burning from the top, progressing slowly downwards. Now and again, a piece would fall to the deck and start to set fire to the wooden deck. However, we were

allowed to put that new fire out each time. The big brute of a man that was their leader said.

'You should have stopped when we first told you. We do not want to harm you or destroy your boat or property. The cargo you carry was taken from those who worked hard to collect it from the earth, and you did not earn it; you just took it from them. These goods belong to all of humanity, and we have as much right to them as you have, so we are taking them now.'

They did not take it all; they just left that small pile of valuables on the deck in front of us.

When they had taken most of our valuables, they boarded their big black boats and left without harming us further. We were losing the battle with our burning sail and mast until Antonio helped us extinguish it. If he had not, then our whole ship might have burned."

The Hittite boat needed help to move without sails and a damaged mast. They still had oars, but they were a long way from the nearest land or port and with wearied and injured crew, that boat was effectively dead in the water. Ladra offered to take them to Sardinia by tying the three ships together, but the captain was very fearful of Sardinia and asked if he could just be taken the much closer distance to the coast. There, there were settlements, and once they were safely attached to a pier, they would soon seek other people to help them repair their boat.

This Ladra and Antonio did, and they watched as the stricken ship rowed the last few hundred metres to a newly constructed small pier covered by curious settlers, many of whom wanted to help. As they left the coast behind them, the two ships continued together. This time they sailed on together, without racing, to Sardinia.

The long diversion to help the Hittite ship took them away from their planned route, which meant that Ladra and Antonio missed the main fleet and were the last to reach Sardinia. The other captains were worried and were preparing to find their missing people when they saw the familiar outline of their missing boats, and they could stop worrying.

Kallisti was delighted to see Antonio and Ladra, and he immediately invited them to stay with them while their ships were being restocked and their crews entertained and rested. His granddaughter made them a fine meal which they all ate seated around Kallisti's elegant table. Antonio told his old mentor about the incident with the pirates. He described in some detail what had happened, but he made sure that he did not mention the mirrors. When he finished, Antonio said there were a couple of things he did not understand, so he asked Kallisti.

"The pirates said they did not want to hurt the crew or their boat, yet they took most of their valuable cargo. They also said that the cargo on the boat did not belong to the Hittites and that they had as much right to it as they did. Can you explain these apparently conflicting statements?"

Kallisti became much more solemn as he started to speak.

"Some of the pirates are of Scythian background..."

This brought a gasp of surprise from Ladra, and he was about to defend the Scythian honour, but his respect for

Kallisti made him hold his tongue, at least until Kallisti had finished. Kallisti paused for a moment and then continued.

"They still carry many Scythian values. They will not harm anyone unless they are at war with them. They will not deliberately damage anyone else's property unless necessary and will always offer retribution. Tell me, did they leave some valuables behind?

Antonio answered.

"They did, but they still stole most of it. That is against the Scythian values."

Kallisti asked another question.

"Did the pirates leave enough to pay for any repairs to the ship?"

Again, Antonio answered.

"Yes, it could have paid for the repairs, but the pirates still stole most of the valuables!"

Kallisti then posed a further series of questions to his guests.

"In Affreidg, who owned the land, the rocks, the water, the trees, or the air?"

Ladra, the Affreidgian, answered this question as accurately as he could.

"Nobody and everybody. It all belongs to Api. It is available for anyone who has a use for it.

But once someone takes it and makes it into something else, it belongs to that man. That is because he has put a piece of himself into that item he has made, his design, expertise, or work. If a man takes a rock and makes an axe, then the axe belongs to that man who made it."

"Exactly so; it belongs to the man who made it."

Said Kallisti with a wry smile on his face. He then asked his next question.

"If I stole that axe head that you mentioned, who does it rightfully belong to?"

Both guests answered together with a tone that implied that the question had an obvious answer.

"The man who made it!

"Exactly so; it belongs to the man who made it."

Repeated Kallisti, and then he asked his third question.

"Who made the goods that were removed from the boat? The captain, the crew, did they make them?

Ladra again answered but realised that this discussion was going differently than he expected.

"No, they did not make them. The new settlers on the mainland made them."

Rather than let Kallisti wind up this discourse, he added.

"But the settlers gave these goods to the captain and crew."

Kallisti immediately returned with a further question, which he promptly answered himself.

"What did the settlers receive in exchange for these goods? Remember that they had already paid the price of their passage out.

*Answer – **nothing**!*

*Those Hittites expect to be paid forever after accepting money for transporting those settlers to a place nobody owned. That is not a bargain. That, my friends, is exploitation, which **is** clearly against Scythian values."*

Ladra thought back to the unfair trading forced on Angus when he had to exchange low-value pots for high-value axes. He thought then that Angus was being exploited, and he played his part in correcting that injustice. Kallisti was right. Those settlers on virgin lands should not have been exploited in such a way. What would he do if a boat landed in Wexford and just demanded money for his just being there and living there?

Kallisti had allowed time for Ladra to collect his thoughts before he asked his following questions and answered them also.

"Who did the pirates harm?

The settlers? Surely not. The Hittites had already harmed them; they had taken the goods from the settlers without a fair bargain. Or did they harm the Hittites, who had taken, those goods from the settlers without a fair deal?

The pirates' goods left on the deck would pay for the repairs to the ship, and the Scythian ninth law of retribution was, therefore, fully satisfied.

Are you stealing goods from someone if that person has already stolen those same goods from someone else? I think not!

Kallisti then went on to further justify the pirate's action.

"Those pirates will now take those goods and spend them in settlements, and in many cases, the same settlements from which they were originally stolen. That then helps the settlements grow by supplying services and goods to the pirates. Just as we do here in Sardinia."

Kallisti had just delivered his coup de grâce. He then sat back with a grin on his face.

Ladra and Antonio knew there was something wrong or immoral about such behaviour, but Kallisti's reasoning was entirely in line with ancient Scythian law. The best argument they had left was that it was wrong for the pirates to benefit from the Hittite exploitation of the settlers.

The best the duo could think of to explain the situation was the ancient Scythian phrase.

'On the backs of dogs are fleas that bite them, and on each of those fleas are lessor fleas to bite them in turn!'

One thought was shared by all of the captains sitting at that table: that the sea now had perils instigated by men, as well as the gods of old. A new dark veil was now cast by the acts of some men on the already dangerous high seas.

The discussion changed; they talked about Antonio, Banba and other domestic matters. But after a few more minutes, Kallisti returned to the subject of the pirates. There was something niggling him that had set up warning bells, but he did not want to make them evident to his friends, his guests.

"How did the pirates stop the Hittite boat? They move fairly fast, and they would be tough to board while moving at speed in the sea."

Ladra and Antonio had not mentioned the mirrors because they both suspected they had been made in Sardinia and did not want to embarrass Kallisti. Ladra now gave a complete description of the mirrors and how they were used in response to the direct question asked.

Kallisti's demeanour changed completely. He went red in the face and became very cross.

*"**Balor**! That scoundrel. That fool!"*

Kallisti could not even find the words to express what he was feeling. He went on.

"Now he has ruined it. This must be reported to the Sardinian council!"

Ladra and Antonio just stayed quiet for the next few minutes. The news had upset their host, and there was nothing they could do or say to help the situation. They had suspected Balor when they first heard about the three black ships, but just a few seconds before, Kallisti connected this piracy act to Balor.

Kallisti muttered to himself before turning his attention once more to his guests. He was not sure what he was going to say to them. Secrecy and not talking about their everyday business details with others was paramount; that was true throughout Sardinia. But this case was different, his people had been deceived as well, and they had been made part of something that went against their moral code. He decided to tell them the problem that had now been raised by the news they had just told him.

"This is Balor's home port. We see him here regularly, and he spends a lot of money on our businesses every few weeks. He is a popular Scythian, a bit rough around the edges but aren't we all? He is a popular leader and well-respected by his men. They would follow him anywhere. They are a very mixed crew from all parts of the world that we know of, and I suspect a few places that we don't. Every one of them would lay down their life for him if needed; I have never before seen such willing dedication to a captain.

But he has gone too far this time, and we have all been deceived by him – he lied to us – he has broken our code here in Sardinia. The Sherden will be furious, and their reputation as fair traders will be ruined!

He asked us to make those extra-large mirrors because the smaller ones, he said, were hard to see in the poor light of some of the very northern seas. We believed him and made them to his specification; he paid us well for them. But we would never have made them if we even suspected him of using them as a weapon. But to use our sun that the gods gave us from their love, for light, heat, and for life, to use that holy light for destruction and even possibly murder; that goes too far!

We would never make anything that would harm any people at sea. We rely on ships and visitors for our livelihood, and if word got out that we had made weapons to destroy boats and from a distance, our reputation would be ruined, and our business would be gone."

Kallisti was still very annoyed and had just said more than his Sardinian code permitted, but his disbelief at what he knew had happened had temporarily suspended reality. He became settled as he thought deeply about what to do next.

Ladra and Antonio just looked at each other without either man saying a word. Then they looked at Kallisti, who was in a trance as his thoughts and mind were not in the same place.

Ladra turned to the granddaughter, who also looked upset, and he thanked her for the great meal and evening and told her that they would return in the morning before they left to say goodbye. They did thank Kallisti, but they, in return, received nothing other than a perfunctory but polite reply.

As they were walking back down to their boats, Antonio said.

"We thought Balor might have been the 'big' pirate, and we suspected that that sun weapon might have been made here, but I never expected that reaction from a hardened man like Kallisti."

"Nor did I! I think Balor may be banished from yet another country.

I wonder where he will go now?"

Replied Ladra, and then after a few seconds.

"It's a shame; he is not that bad of a guy. I knew him as a child, you know. He was brought up near my tribe, along with Cessair and me.

He was a bit of a bully, using his strength and size at every opportunity. He just upped and left one morning without any notice or explanation. He does have his good points, however, and he is a man of some principle. But he is his worst enemy; he has little sense of balance. He goes a little too far in everything and always crosses that imaginary line of decency.

He has become a leader, one way or another; otherwise, his crew would not follow him the way they do. Strangely I feel sorry for him and his chosen path!"

The two continued in silence for a while before Ladra spoke again.

"We will have to find a way to defeat or avoid that weapon that Balor now has!"

The rest of the walk down to their boats was in silence.

Partholon's Story.

Partholon was by far the youngest brother in his family. He was not expected to be the tribe leader, nor had he the natural disposition to be a warrior. His tribe, however, was one of the largest tribes in Affreidg and its leader was very influential within the Great Tribal Council. As a child, he had no straightforward life planned for him, and he drifted from one thing to the next. He was smart enough but lacked the focus and drive to achieve his as-yet-unknown desires and goals.

He spent part of his youth exploring the seas of Affreidg, and then he explored, with Ladra, the Mediterranean. He found that, like Ladra, he enjoyed boats, but he enjoyed trading more. His family thought both were a little beneath him and that he was wasting his time pursuing these interests. He married young, yet he still lacked ambition for his future. That was until the great flood came, and everybody's world changed.

Sera, his father, was a powerful man. He did not take fools lightly, yet his thinking was entrenched, old-fashioned and a little foolish; he never saw it that way. In his father's eyes, Partholon had never proved himself, and in some sense, he was seen by his family as a bit of a disappointment. When Partholon went off exploring, sometimes for many months, his father was glad that he was not reminded of his son's apparent shortcomings daily. He frequently used to complain to his wife about their youngest son.

"Why can't Partholon learn from and become more like his eldest brother Greecius?

The flood changed everything for all Affreidgians, but Cessair's simple request changed Partholon's future and his way of living forever.

Sera had such a large tribe that he split them into three groups. The largest group was to be led by the eldest son Greecius. He was to take his tribe to Thrace and merge them with the unorganised group of people already living there. The rest of Sera's tribe was too big to travel together to Babylon, so Partholon took some of them and shadowed his father on their way there.

Partholon would never forget that day on the mountainside in Affreidg when he watched Ardfear and the massive ark being carried high on the top of a gigantic wave. It was being borne, safely in Tabiti's hands, to a new life, a new future, and a new world. It was an electrifying experience that reached deep into his soul and lit a fire to forge his moral fibre. Never before in his young life had he felt as he did at that moment. He knew that he had a purpose in life, that he too could make a difference – but he still did not know what it was or how he would do it.

It worried him so much that he did not even join in with the celebratory party that night; he knew that he was a vital cog, but he did not know where he fits into Tabiti's plan. His long-time friend Cessair was already a tribe leader, and she had an important role to play, and she was getting on with it. He went to bed early that night, and despite encouragement from his loving wife, his spirits were extremely low.

There is a famous saying, '*What a difference a day makes,*' but for Partholon, the difference came overnight.

Very early the following day, an old friend came crashing into his tent. Ladra just barged in and shook Partholon awake with no manners, decorum, or tact. Anyone else would not have come within yards of the tent before he would have been challenged and stopped, but Ladra was so frequent a visitor that he was considered as one of the family. Ladra was excited, still pumped up with the experiences of the previous few days – he just blurted out the words.

"Wake up! Wake up! Partholon! Cessair needs you. She needs you now!"

To have anyone say that they '*need you*' is a powerful motivator, and for Cessair, the chosen young new leader, to need him, Partholon, just made the motivation even stronger. His astute wife, Elgnat, was also rudely woken by Ladra's actions. She quickly assessed the possibilities and encouraged her husband with the words.

"Go quickly, dear. Listen to what she has to say. This may well change our lives."

How right she was!

A couple of hours later, he returned a man with conviction. Elgnat had guessed correctly, and she wholly agreed with his newly proposed plans. This was an excellent opportunity for their family and the section of their tribe.

Cessair had asked Partholon to accompany her to find new lands for all their tribes. Ladra would help him to build his boats and to start his own trading business. Hippolyte would keep them safe with her mounted warriors. It was now time for Partholon and his family to take control of their lives and to follow their friends down their own path and into their own future.

Sera, his father, was dubious at first and even started to dismiss Partholon's new plans as nonsensical, but as his newfound passion, and more importantly, his commitment came over, Sera came around to the idea that Partholon should 'cut the apron strings,' and take his section of the tribe and leave.

Partholon had thought out an intelligent and considered plan; what is more, he had been specifically picked by the best of company. Young as she was, Cessair had great judgement in people and was going far. Sera was even a little disappointed that she had not made the same offer to him. He would have gone with her; if she had asked him!

He now saw his youngest son for the first time in a new light. Sera, at last, saw him as an intelligent leader in the making.

A couple of hours later, he watched Partholon lead his people up the steep hill to catch up with Cessair, Hippolyte, and their tribes. He was saddened by his leaving, especially now that he only just saw him in that new way, but he was immensely proud of this young man, his son.

In the company of Cessair and her allies, Partholon found confidence and experience in 'bucket loads.' After only a couple of days of joining Cessair, the overnight dash to save the Hittite abductees from becoming enslaved people at the hand of Balor's raiding party, his total success that night, gave him confidence. He could also become a true leader without looking over his shoulder for his father's approval. Shortly afterwards, his raid with Matanni to travel to Thrace to recover Hittite slaves that had been already captured forced him to see the reality behind the power of his big brother, the apple of his father's eye. Then, there, in his brother's palace, he stood up to his powerful elder brother for the first time. He had won the day; he won it by using intellect, not by brute force. While this was a bloodless and minor incident, it was an important event between siblings. That raid started a discord between the Hittites and the Greeks that would last for millennia and cost countless lives.

Alongside Hatti's tribe, Partholon established Caria, a settlement that grew and flourished in their new lands near Troy. Partholon left Elgnat and his family behind when he travelled to Sidon. He went with Ladra to help build Ladra's great ships, and he was soon able, with Ladra's assistance, to create a trading fleet for himself. Like Ladra, he became on good trading terms with the Phoenicians and was crucial to Ladra's profitable trade and haulage of Lebanon's timber to Egypt.

The new Black Sea was full three years after he left the flooding Affreidg. The great deafening roar of the incoming cascading waters, which dominated the demise of Affreidg, had abated in only a few months, but the strong currents continued for many more. The small part of Partholon's tribe that he had left religiously guarding and waiting to float Ladra's beached boat had not wasted their time. They had been joined by many more who liked the idea of being part of this patient but forward-looking group, and during that time, Partholon's small rear guard became a thriving settlement. They had not only built houses but also copied Ladra's boat and produced two more.

When the strong currents in the Black Sea finally stopped, a group of self-trained sailors headed out to find Partholon and the rest of their tribe. They stayed close to the new coast, only making a few miles daily. They were the first to sail out of the Black Sea into the Sea of Marmara. They were apprehensive when they entered the first artificial port they had seen; they had just taken their most considerable risk. They were, however, relieved and delighted when the first words that they heard were Scythian, for they had just sailed into the new port of Troy.

When Cessair left to foster Scotia in Egypt, Partholon was left to grow and mature his trading business. His 'rear-guard' were the first boats of his fleet to travel between his old world and his new one. Soon trading with his former compatriots in Affreidg became big business, and his ships were quickly joined by Magog's, and all their combined trade was handled in Troy by Partholon.

While Cessair was in Meroe, dozens of tribes, who had tried to make a new life in Babylon, realised their future was not there. When Babel's tower collapsed along with the structure of society in Babylon, the trickle of tribes leaving became a second exodus. Many wanted to travel with Cessair on her quest to find her new land, but many others just wanted to find any new land to call home.

Partholon's Story.

Hatti and Matanni had started rehousing many of these tribes, but at a great price. They charged for their passage to a new land and forced an agreement from them that the new settlers would pay a substantial regular tribute and that it would be paid to Hatti forever! This was entirely against Scythian principles, but Hatti was not a Scythian and Matanni, now his sidekick, had forsaken much of his Scythian heritage.

When Cessair returned from Meroe and started to move her tribes to Ériu, it was Partholon who continued to organise the logistics at Troy. When it became time for a new tribe to be transported to Ériu, Partholon prepared them and handled the property they left behind.

But many new tribes continued to arrive from Babylon, but they did not want to travel as far as Ériu, nor did they trust or want to pay Hatti for his expensive services. Partholon and his trading business were doing very well, and his next move was as shrewd as it was wise. He would transport these homeless tribes to new lands for free if they agreed to primarily trade with him when they became established.

His problem was that many of the larger local islands had already been settled by Hatti and Hatti almost had a monopoly of the best sites. The little islands and lands south of Thrace were best suited to small, isolated communities with few communication routes between them. Only Sicily offered the best chance for much larger tribes. It was large, with not many people living there. Furthermore, he had learnt that Gomer had just settled other Scythian tribes in Italy, which were not far away.

It was not long before Partholon moved Elgnat and the rest of his family to Sicily to make it their home, far away from the developing war with his brother. His brother lived in the country he had taken over and renamed after himself; Greece was just across the sea from Troy.

When Ladra arrived in Troy with his fleet, Partholon stood on the quay to welcome him with a big smile and shouted the words.

"Welcome back, Ladra. I thought that Cessair was going to keep you in Ériu forever.

It had been a few years since the two lifelong friends had met, and they both had missed each other's company. Ladra replied as he clambered down to the pier and joined his friend.

"Glad to be back, my friend. I have missed the calm Mediterranean and the warm sea. You have made great changes here. How the port has grown; so many new piers; you must be busy!"

Partholon's Story.

The two friends continued their close relationship as though the intervening years had not existed.

Partholon then took Ladra to his house. But first, he told his men to secure the ships, unload them and prepare them for loading with the next tribes. Ladra's crew needed time to rest, to reinvigorate themselves before their long and hazardous return trip to Ériu. Winter was not far away, and time could not be wasted, as with every passing day towards winter, the seas would become more dangerous.

When they arrived at Partholon's accommodation, he expected to see Elgnat and the rest of the family. Still, the house was almost lifeless, except for a couple of hired serving girls and general help that is so necessary around a busy man's house. Ladra asked the obvious question.

"Where are Elgnat and the rest of your family?"

Partholon cheery mood evaporated, and his tone dried as he spoke.

"I took them to Sicily for their safety."

Ladra gasped slightly while the problem was told to him.

"Greecius never got over my raid to rescue the Hittites. He was affronted that I should have made such a fool of him, especially in front of all his people. He is said to have sworn vengeance on me and the Hittites and that we would pay with our lives. In the meantime, he has become power crazy, just like Saball's son and, for that matter, Hatti and Matanni. All of them have realised that if they subdue other peaceful peoples, they can extract wealth without work. They, in their ways, are becoming international bullies.

It all started when Saball's power-crazy son sent chariots to subdue the neighbouring countries. Hatti and Matanni did not use military force but did the same thing by using unfair business deals. Hatti's empire, and that is what it is now, stretches to the Pillars of Hercules. They all pay him tributes for just settling in their new homes. Hatti's empire covers many Mediterranean islands; now, many of his settlements are on that sea's northern coast.

Greecius, fired by his takeover of Northern Thrace, is also rapidly expanding beyond the official boundaries. He is using a combination of settlement and trade. When he is not accepted, as is often the case, he uses force to subdue the country.

Saball's son, who is not yet Pharoah, though I hear he soon will be, is jealously watching Hatti's expansion. Not to be outdone, he is racing his chariots all along the southern Mediterranean coast, subduing every country in his way. Our world is going mad! Money and trading are changing everything.

I fear it will not be long before the former allies, the Hittites and the Egyptians, will fight over distant lands. Hatti and Greecius have already started in some islands off Greece."

Ladra listened, dumbfounded. He had only been away a short time, but in that time, the whole world seemed mad. He was not even sure what to say or to ask. He didn't need to because Partholon continued his tale of woe.

Partholon's Story.

"I moved my family to Sicily because I believe that this place will soon become too dangerous to live – we here are too close to Greece."

Ladra suspected that his friend had not told him the whole story of why he had moved his family, and it soon became evident that he was right in his suspicions. Partholon demeanour hardened a steelier look developed in his eye when he started to talk again.

"Greecius is going too far! Our father moved the rest of our tribe after the collapse of Babylon. He has moved to join Greecius in Greece. I hear that he is in the palace, but like Saball, he has no say or power over his tribe anymore; Greecius has taken over completely. I cannot stand by and just let this happen."

This threat of action by Partholon against Greece would have dire consequences, and it would undoubtedly jeopardise Cessair's mission of transporting all her people from Troy to Ériu. He could not stay quiet any longer, so he blurted out.

"But you promised Cessair that you would help her get all her people to Ériu. You cannot do that if you are fighting with your brother!"

"Don't worry."

Was Partholon's quick reply.

"The next couple of years will see all of Cessair's tribes safely in Ériu. That is, if you continue at the same rate you

have been moving them. I will not do anything against Greecius until all of Cessair's people are safely in Ériu."

Partholon's final words on the subject came from his soul.

"But then, I have a duty to my father and the wider tribe."

To try and lighten the mood and enjoy his friend's company and hospitality, Ladra asked.

*"Is there any **good** news? Are any decent people benefitting during all this unrest?*

Partholon's reply was swift and emphatic.

"The Phoenicians! They are raking it in from all sides.

They have little or no territory, so no one wants to invade them. They supply everyone with goods that the big empires are not equipped or capable of getting for themselves. The Egyptians do not even have ships capable of sailing beyond the Nile, so they hire the Phoenicians for everything except fighting. They used the Phoenicians to supply and collect goods from the countries that they conquered. The Hittites also used them for trade as the Hittite empire was mainly limited around the Mediterranean, and when they needed goods from further afield. The Greeks also trade extensively with the Phoenicians.

Partholon's Story.

Everybody knows that the Phoenicians are not a threat to them and at the same time that without them trading, all of their burgeoning economies would collapse. "

"Anyone else benefit from all of this turmoil? "

Asked Ladra. He was fishing for news about Partholon's business empire. But he was surprised by Partholon's following answer.

"Balor, among others! They have become warriors for hire, and Egypt is hiring. Saball's son has no one to fight at sea, so he hires sea traders to fight for him. I think that it did not work out too well for Balor. He was bad at following orders as an Egyptian paid sea warrior. "

After the shock of hearing Balor's name so soon after Sardinia, Ladra laughed at the thought of Balor, the Egyptian sea warrior – that he did not expect. He laughed again when he realised that there was yet another country in which Balor was not welcome. The laughter about their erstwhile compatriot lightened the mood for both of them, and the rest of the evening became much more pleasant, and they exchanged news of each other's successes while apart.

It was the next day before Ladra and Partholon discussed business. They were looking at the large pile of copper ore sitting close to the pier, having been recently unloaded. Partholon said.

"There is much copper in that ore. It is of very high quality. "

Then he looked at the 'ingots' of smelted copper that Fintan had already extracted from the ore and said.

"Now, those are valuable! There is a huge demand for a product of that quality. I could sell that for a great price. Bring me all that you can make of that I could easily sell it all."

Ladra was wise enough not to commit all of Ériu's products as he knew that the world and its markets were growing daily. Ladra was unsure whether it was his imagination or just a couple of 'off' days, but Partholon had changed slightly. Hardly perceptible, but something was different. Fun-loving, life first, Partholon was becoming a 'hard-nosed' businessman. His life priorities were changing, and the importance of business and status were creeping to the top.

Ladra's visit was shorter than expected. The current group of emigrating tribes had been enthusiastic about moving and prepared well for the trip. Partholon was, by now, well-practised in processing so many people and provisioning the ships quickly. It would have been foolish to delay their departure unnecessarily, and so, only a few days after he had arrived, Ladra was again on board and leaving Troy.

Balor, the son of Dot, was born in Affreidg. Dot, the master builder, was a giant of a man capable of lifting rocks that generally took two men to handle and building them securely into a strong wall. He had a good reputation as a builder and was always the man to whom the tribe went if a large and robust building was needed.

Balor entered this world a large baby, and his whole tribe had never seen a baby of his size, and for a while, the news of this enormous child circulated all around Affreidg. He remained large as a toddler, and for much of his very early life, he was the size of a child of twice his age. Dot was constantly told that Balor would be the next master builder; if he continued to be so large, he might even surpass his father in strength.

At first, Balor enjoyed playing with the other children his age, and Balor had a very happy childhood for the first few years. He was very gentle and did not even realise that he was much stronger than his peers. But one important day, when Balor was still an infant, an incident happened that would change the course of his life.

He was playing with some toy, and another small child just took Balor's favourite toy from him and started to play with it himself. Balor just sat down and cried at the loss of **his** toy.

Dot and many others saw the whole incident, so Dot admonished his son for letting the other child take his toy from him. Dot was embarrassed that people would laugh at his large son having his toy taken by so small a boy, he said.

"Balor, that was your toy. It would be best if you had not let that little boy take it from you. You are much bigger than him. Just be a man and go and get it back! In this world, you must take back what was yours."

Balor did precisely what his father had told him to do. In front of everyone, he purposefully walked over to the small child who was holding the taken toy. He grabbed it and pulled it from the smaller boy's hands. The small boy also liked the toy, so he kept it tightly. Balor held the toy resolutely and firmly pushed the other boy away. Balor was excited, and he had not judged his strength correctly. The small boy not only fell to the ground but also rolled over backwards two or three times; the small child then burst into a flood of tears.

Balor proudly held on firmly to his favourite toy. The other boy was not hurt beyond the shock of the swift retribution for stealing in the first place. But for Balor, the feeling of pleasure he had of having his favourite toy safely back in his hands was incredible and the only thing that mattered.

Many of the onlookers would not have taken much notice of the childhood incident, except that this child was Balor, the giant child, the child that pushed the smaller child, and he used such force. Soon the word spread that the Balor boy was using his size to take what he wanted. Many of his age group were told to stay away from him in case they would be hurt. This news spread, and Balor's bullying reputation grew.

Balor's Story.

As Balor grew older, he tried to participate in games
with the other children, but all too often, when they
nervously showed reluctance to let him join in, he would
lose patience with waiting and would barge in and take part.
The game would then break up, the children separated, and
they blamed him for spoiling their fun. This only made his
reputation worse.

Later a group of older boys befriended him because he
was the strongest, and they found that they could make fun
with him as their 'leader' and protector. This often took the
form of annoying and teasing those children who formally
would not play with them. Balor did not enjoy teasing or
bullying the other children, but he was the leader of his gang,
and every time he bullied some unfortunate child, his
'followers' had more lavish praise for him, making him feel
good. In time, the bullying became easier for him, and his
gang's admiration of his bravado sustained his ego.

Ladra was a friend to Balor when he was around; both had so few friends. Ladra was obsessed with boats and was frequently away on long journeys. Sometimes Ladra would let Balor travel with him on his boat for short trips, and Balor liked that. It was something in the power of the water that resonated with Balor, for Balor, his favourite god, had to be Thagimasidas, the god of the sea.

As a young teenager, life became exceedingly difficult when his adult hormones started to race through his body. His attraction to the girls of his tribe completely hit him sideways. This interest was new to him, and he was unprepared for this phase of his life. He had learned from an early age that strength was might. That the strongest won – the rest lost. He had never been just a member of a team that didn't jockey for leadership and control, and he could not understand the concept or even how such a group could exist without a single strong and, above all, dominant leader. He was the strongest of his gang, and therefore he should get the first choice in anything as he was their leader. In his eyes, Tabiti had made men stronger, which implied that she made man to lead and dominate women. Following his young logic, the weaker sex was destined by Tabiti to be the lesser sex.

There was one girl in his tribe that did not fit in with Balor's understanding of Tabiti's apparent rules of life. Cessair was nothing like as strong as him physically, and she should not have even registered with him and his values that were based on physical strength, but she was different! There was something special about this girl, something he did not yet understand. For years, he had tried to show her his strength; usually, that would have been enough to have anyone show him their respect; but with Cessair, she just laughed at his efforts. The more he tried to show her that he had become a man, the more she made him feel like a little boy.

Balor became obsessed with Cessair and started to think about her day and night. Often at night, he would lie awake thinking.

"Why will Cessair not see how strong I am? She still sees me as a little boy. If she truly saw the man I have become, she would love me and be proud to be with the man who will soon be the strongest in Affreidg!"

He could not see that his obsession was taking control of him and the only goal in his sheltered life was to own Cessair and bring her into his life, much as he had that favourite toy all those years ago. The only way that he thought that this could be achieved was by strength.

His obsession with Cessair grew, and he became jealous whenever he saw her with Ladra. He could not understand why she should like him. Ladra was not as strong as him; he spent so much time on boats, and she didn't particularly like boats.

One evening when he was intensely frustrated in his mission to win Cessair and was at a loss as to what to do, he passed two much older men digging a pit in the ground. Balor knew what it was for, and he started to help them. He helped them gather the large rocks to pile on the fire he had built. They called him a man because he had brought the largest stones to the party. He joined them around the fire while it roared and was given a little fermented grape while they took a lot more. When the fire died down, and they erected the tent over the piping-hot rocks, it should have been time for Balor to go. The older men had taken too much to drink, so when Balor asked to join them in the tent, they only said that the tent was for men only. Balor pointed out that he had carried the largest rocks, so he was as much of a man as they were. Balor's logic made sense in their 'fogged' minds, so he entered the tent with them.

The fumes emitted from the seeds, which had been cast onto the hot rocks, loosened their tongues, inhibitions, and sensibility. After a few minutes, Balor became lightheaded, his senses heightened, and his emotions surfaced. He was in tears, complaining bitterly.

"I like that girl Cessair. But every time I try and approach her and show her that I have become a strong man, she makes me feel like a little boy, and then she leaves!

By this time, the two men thought that they were in the zone of the gods, and one of them half-heartily replied.

"Show her that you are a man!"

With that, the men passed out and left Balor to his deepening thoughts. Balor could take the fumes no more, so he staggered out of the tent into the evening air. He looked up, and right in front of him was his obsession, his Cessair, his nemesis.

The fumes of the tent tainted his thoughts, and his logic abandoned him. He thought.

"If I just hold her tight, and she sees how strong of a man I am and how much I want her, she will be bound to see and love me."

In Balor's mind, the logic was sound; all he had to do was put his perfect plan into action. He did not realise the fumes impaired his mind or that his body was also. As he stepped forward to grab Cessair, he stumbled, and he and Cessair fell in a heap on the ground.

The next few seconds were a blur, and he was not sure exactly what happened, but she had just put a knife against his throat, and he was now running away.

When he rested awhile, and the effects of the fumes had worn off, he realised just what he had done. He had gone too far and realised that now so clearly. She obviously did not love him; she had taken out her knife and might have killed him. He was shocked at himself and annoyed that he had made her fear for her life so intensely that she took such action to defend herself. He could no longer be trusted around her; he just had to leave Affreidg.

He never told his gang what happened with Cessair that night, but he still persuaded them that it was time for them all to leave Affreidg and become men.

Once in Thrace, Balor and his friends travelled south until he reached a town by the sea. He could easily find work there because of his size and strength. His friends were considered as much younger. They weren't. They were, however, allowed to work alongside their much bigger and older-looking colleague, Balor. There were no constraints put on this formidable group of boisterous adolescents. No work was refused if it paid well. With money to burn and no family or tribe to curb their excessiveness, they went wild, doing whatever they wanted without a care, with impunity.

The people of Thrace already believed in the 'natural' superiority of the male sex, and that fitted well with Balor's beliefs that he already held. His gang's excesses and disregard for social norms quickly alienated them from the bulk of ordinary 'decent' people. This, however, did not worry Balor's group because they always found well-paid 'dirty' work. Many people crowded around them, and they were always new 'friends' only too willing to help Balor spend his new wealth doing whatever he wanted or desired!

Balor worked hard and, to his credit, despite his wild lifestyle, earned a reputation as a hard and diligent worker. By far, the best-paying jobs for his skills were to be found at the docks. The Phoenician trading ships would arrive and dock. From the moment they arrived, the longer the boat stayed at the pier, the more time the traders wasted. The boats had to be unloaded and reloaded with traded goods as quickly as possible. Fit solid young men like Balor's gang commanded a premium price; they held back the valuable ships and crew with the least costly waiting time.

Sometimes the trading boats had to unload and reload at different local ports. If this was the case, then Balor's men often went with the ships to carry the goods aboard, and they were then dropped off as the boats passed back past the original port. Balor loved these trips and knew he wanted to spend more time on board.

The day the earth shook, Balor was almost killed as the building he was in fell all around him. He was lucky, but some of his friends were injured, and others died. Many in that town died that day as the town was reduced to rubble in only minutes. Balor's strength allowed him to rescue many people buried alive, and the townsfolk admired his caring deeds. He saw the world differently from that day onwards.

He did his part in rebuilding the town and showed many of the building skills he had learnt from his father. He was starting to grow and mature, and he was beginning to make a useful life for himself. Then Greecius arrived.

Greecius arrived with many thousands of people and took control of the country. The free and easy Thracians now had a dictator as a leader, and they had become second-class citizens to the invading Scythians. But Greecius did not bring with him the true Scythian values but instead set up his own set built upon privilege. Balor found himself torn between his new compatriots, where he had now been accepted and respected as a hard-working citizen, and his Scythian blood that classed him as the same as the 'first-class' invaders.

Greecius soon found that all of the preinvasion people of Thrace were needed to keep the country running and to produce essentials such as food. He wanted to forge a new country based on strength, class and intellect, and this new country was to be named after him. He and his elite class needed people to do the essential menial tasks that would allow him to have a high standard of living.

Balor, the Scythian, the strong worker, the man who would do any 'dirty' job for money, was summoned to the palace and set before Greecius, the new king. Greecius cleared the room of everyone but Balor, and he spoke to him directly.

"We are building a great new country here, and I know that across the sea, there are people who were also devastated by the earth-shaking. Many want to come here and have a great new life in our strong new country. Their king will not let them move to a better life, and he uses his army to keep them as prisoners in their villages.

I want you to bring as many as you can to freedom here, and when you do, I will pay you handsomely for each man, woman, or child you save. I will make you a rich and powerful man, and, as a Scythian, you will become important in my court.

This must be done in the greatest secrecy; tell no one about this. This is so their cruel leader, or his spies, do not learn of our plan and lie in ambush. You must go at night and not be seen. I have already arranged boats for this mercy mission."

Balor could not believe his luck; the king had personally asked him to help these poor unfortunate neighbouring people escape to a great new and productive life in a modern go-ahead country. He had been given charge of fine boats with captains and crews, and he could pick his men.

The first few mercy missions went very well. The 'cruel' leader did have a few men that fought hard, but Balor still succeeded. Strangely the people did not seem to be happy about being saved from their squalid conditions and brought to Greece. He knew they would soon see how good a life they could have in Greece, a vibrant country with a strong king.

The king did not pay him at first, but his wealth was building up and was in the safekeeping of the king. Only one more trip and his fortune would be realised. The last 'mercy' trip for the king was also to be the last trip for the king.

When Balor arrived on that final excursion, he was starting to wonder if the people he saved were better off in Greece. It had been several months since his first expedition, and none of the people he had already saved seemed happy. They did not seem to have an easy life. He had found it difficult when he first arrived there until he found his place, but somehow, they were different; they didn't seem to grow to like the area as he had.

Once the 'rescued' people were safe aboard that day, he thought that he and his crew would spend the night in the Hittite village to celebrate their last trip and the prospect of collecting his fortune from the king. There was something wrong about this whole mercy mission that he did not easily understand. He had, after all, been sent by the king himself. His childhood conditioning to bullying made him slow to see what was happening, but an uneasiness settled on him, and he was glad that this was his last trip.

That night while sitting in that foreign hovel, he told his friends.

"I am glad that this is our last trip. I am not sure our new king is as good as we thought. I am not sure if I want to live under his rule. When we return to Greece, I will collect my money from Greecius, buy a boat, and start trading. I would like that. Do you think that the king would let me buy one of these boats? Will any of you come with me?

A chorus of men all agreed, and he had more than enough for a crew.

The following day, he was captured by Hippolyte and her women. The ignominy of being captured by that woman.

What made it worse was that he knew that, in her eyes, his life was of no value and that she would gladly dispatch him with a single mechanical stroke. Then he saw Cessair, the girl he left Affreidg for, the woman that he had wanted to possess. She now owned his life and had judgement over his future. When he heard Cessair's words, said in disgust and disappointment, he wished that Hippolyte had made that swift but fatal stroke. She had asked him.

"Balor! How could you? Why?"

Cessair had spared his life without even listening to his story. He had been relegated to a small island close to his home port in Greece; Partholon had just dumped him and his men there. That was just before they raided and took back all the people Balor had been paid to collect. They had been put ashore with food and water but no apparent way to leave.

The trees and animals on the island gave them a method of escape. Balor remembered the small boat that Ladra had made when they were small boys living at the mouth of the Danube. They killed and skinned the animals; they bent a row of saplings over into an upturned 'U', tied the hides on the U form, and made crude but practical boats.

By early morning they had paddled their newly built curraghs, the short distance to the mainland coast. They walked and reached the port just after Partholon had left with the rescued Hittites and most of the stolen Greek boats. Balor spoke with one of his captains.

70

Balor's Story.

"The king will not pay us now. I am sure that after what has just happened, we will all be killed for sure. We must run! But where? How?"

"Look! There are three boats left at the pier."

Said the captain; he went on.

"I am sure Partholon did something to them before they left, but we are captains and crews; we will be able to fix them for sure."

So, while the soldiers were explaining to an angry Greecius all that had happened the night before, Balor and his men quietly sailed the remaining three Greek boats out of that port; they swore never to return to it again.

Balor had learnt the hard way just what it felt like to be manipulated and exploited, and he did not like it. For one of the first times in his life, he understood some of the core tenements of Scythian culture and their non-aggressive way of life.

What had happened to Balor and his men meant that they were not welcome, either in Greecius' lands or in Hatti's, and those were the only areas of the Mediterranean that any of them knew. One of his captains had heard of Sardinia a long way off to the west; it was far away from Greece!

Balor arrived in Sardinia with slight trepidation. They had aimlessly drifted for weeks, not knowing what to do or where to go. One of the captains suggested that the Sherden might accept them for their sailing skills. They had no valuables or food and feared that the news of them having stolen the ships may have already arrived.

There were a few local people as the three large, anonymous boats docked at the pier for the first time. Balor led the crews as they climbed down to meet their unknown hosts. He picked out an older man to talk with, a man with an unmistakable air of having seen most things and one that had the respect of those around him. Balor spoke first.

"We have fled from Greece, and we need help."

"Well, you have come to the right place. You and your crews look exhausted and hungry. You sound more like a Scythian than a Greek.

It was a terrible thing that happened to your country. Send your men for food and rest over there; our people will look after them. You can come with me and tell me the whole story. One Scythian custom I strongly believe in is giving support and sanctuary to all who need it.

My name is Kallisti. What is yours?"

With that generous invitation, Balor went to Kallisti's house. There, the two men were met by Cethlenn: Kallisti's youngest daughter.

Cethlenn quickly prepared a table stocked with the best foods, some of which Balor had never even seen before. While she was showing Balor to his seat, there was a veritable spark between them, and they both nervously laughed. During that meal, strong friendships began, and they would last for the rest of their lives.

Balor told Kallisti everything, right back to the critical incidents of his childhood. He saw Kallisti as a father figure he now knew he had missed. Balor desperately missed the stability, and security of someone he could be himself with, someone he could let see the real Balor. Kallisti, at the same time, saw a young man who had made simple but flawed decisions throughout his life and someone who had lost his moral compass. He needed the help that he had so wisely asked for.

Kallisti was getting too old to lead his small fleet of trading ships. Balor was a strong and capable young man who only lacked direction and the correct type of company.

The two men spent a long time learning about each other before Kallisti turned to Balor and made him an offer he could not refuse.

"I want you to become my apprentice. I will teach you the ways of the sea. I will show you the trading routes and introduce you to my customers. I will work you hard for the next few years, and you may wish you never went to sea with me. You will often hate it; you will be wet and cold. Other times it will be so hot and humid that you wish you were back in the cold. I can promise you that no two days will be the same. I will show you places and things that you will not believe.

*You will, for that time, follow my every command because I will be **your** captain. I will teach you how to lead men. Men should want to follow you, not because they are scared of your great strength, but rather, they should follow you because they feel safe and comfortable doing so; I will teach you that.*

Your crew will become the family and true friends that you never really had. You will learn to rely on them just as they will you."

The two then struck up an agreement. Balor would, in due course, take Kallisti's place in the Sherden fleet, and in return, Balor would share the profits earned with his mentor and business partner, Kallisti.

Kallisti's Trading Routes.

Balor had never really been anyone's apprentice before, and everyone knew that the next couple of years could be difficult. However, Balor had one significant advantage: he knew and was mature enough to ask for help. He liked the life that Kallisti had made for himself, far away from his native land of Santorini. He knew that if he was diligent and hardworking, he could forge a new life and a new home for himself, suggesting a pleasant future.

Kallisti was up for the task ahead of him. Over the years, hundreds of men had passed through his hands, and he had become an excellent judge of character. Balor was a man that stood apart from the masses. He was neither a sheep nor a wolf by natural temperament, and in Kallisti's experience, which was unusual. He felt responsible for his new ward and knew that the next couple of years would set Balor's course for the rest of his life.

Kallisti's first practical task was inspecting Balor's men and boats. The state of the ships would tell him little, as they were only a few weeks in Balor's possession, but the competence of his crew's management during their trip from Greece would show through. The men, however, would tell him a lot more about Balor, as Kallisti knew well that a man could often be judged by the company that he keeps.

Kallisti was uncompromising with his words to Balor.

"You fled from Affreidg. You stole people from the Hittites and ships from the Greeks! Not a great start for a peaceful trader who needs to be friends and trade with everyone. Fortunately, you have not upset the Egyptians or the Phoenicians – Yet!"

75

In the last line, he spoke with a great smile on his face. The smile, however, did not soften the message that Balor needed to blend in, disappear, and be seen as just another trader doing his regular business. Kallisti continued.

"As traders, we do not usually turn up somewhere new and sell a range of products. Most of what is sold has already been agreed upon and priced many months, sometimes years, previously. We create a route that we follow, and we stop at each port to deliver what we had already contracted to supply on our last visit.

You have three magnificent ships, the best ones the Greeks have ever built. You paid yourselves well for the disgusting missions that Greecius hired you for. He deserves to lose them for the pain and suffering that he inflicted on those poor Hittites!

They are much bigger than regular small boats, which can only travel a short distance daily. They must stay close to the shore and can only carry small loads. If you carefully watch the sea, your ships can go anywhere, even beyond the Pillars of Hercules."

Cethlenn brought some drinks and snacks to the two men, that were deep in discussion. Kallisti noted that this was the third time in as many hours. This was unusual, as Cethlenn was usually not so attentive to their guests. A few minutes later, he continued.

"Essential to all trading is trust. Without it, there is no business. Rarely do we leave a port with goods to the value of what we brought in, but after months or years, we should

see our profits. Sometimes we agree to bring several loads of a product during the year, but they only pay us, for it all, with something that they only harvest in one specific month. We have to be there at that port and at the right time to be paid for that product! We then have to rush it to our customers and sell it before it goes off and spoils."

Balor asked.

"Why doesn't everyone just pay with gold?

Kallisti replied.

"Not every country has gold. In countries with gold mines, gold has a value. In countries with no gold mines then, the value is much higher. Take, for example, the rock with copper in it. In Cyprus, it is just another rock; they have so much of it. A shipload of it there has truly little value to them. Here in Sardinia, or Santorini, that same shipload has great value. Transporting that heavy rock is difficult and dangerous; we must profit from carrying it on our valuable ships. That is our business. We have to make everyone, at both ends, feel happy with our deals."

Cethlenn gently interrupted the men to say that it was becoming late in the day and that she needed to go out for some supplies. Balor immediately jumped up and said.

"I will help you carry them."

Kallisti laughed silently to himself when Balor and his daughter left the house together.

It was not long before the ships were once again at sea. Most of Balor's apprenticeship would be at sea, and there would be plenty of time on board to talk about the theory.

Balor had no idea that the world was so large or changed so much from place to place. As the lands changed, so did the people that occupied them. In areas where most people were hunter-gathers, there were no towns or ports and, therefore, little or no trade. But islands tended to be particularly good for business, and every large island with people had a thriving port. The islanders understood that boats could bring, to their islands, commodities or goods that could not be found locally. Traders were always welcome there, and any news or gossip from the outside world was a welcome bonus for an isolated island.

Kallisti worked Balor hard. They travelled all around the Mediterranean and beyond. Sometimes they carried precious jewels such as emeralds mined in Syria and Sheba. They had been carried overland by caravan to ports on the Mediterranean. Other goods, such as ebony or ivory, came from even further afield; they came from India either overland or by other boat traders that travelled through the Red Sea. A prevalent form of 'local' ivory came from the tusks of rhinocerotes that used to roam freely in Affreidg and still did in the eastern countries around the Mediterranean. The best axes and other stone items came from the other end of Kallisti's world. They went from a tiny island off Ériu, many miles north of the Pillars of Hercules.

The best spices from the Arabian Peninsula, textiles from Egypt, Copper ore from Cyprus and wood from the Levant. To Balor, the list seemed endless as every trading port was particularly good at producing something unique to them and highly desirable to everyone else.

Even though the ships were large, they always ensured that they were always in some port or sheltered cove at nightfall. When they could not make a port because it was too far to travel in a day, knowledge of secluded coves or bays was essential for survival. In many ways, it was the knowledge of where the safe mooring places were that were the most important lessons of all.

It was rare that two ships would come close at sea, but each time it was an occasion to learn what was ahead of them.

By the end of his apprenticeship, Kallisti was confident that Balor was a wise investment and capable sailor and trader. His relationship became even closer when Balor married Cethlenn, and they built themselves a house nearby.

For six years, that agreement worked very well. Kallisti stayed in Sardinia and organised many significant innovations, such as lighting the nightly beacon. Balor had found his direction and loved his vocation. He became an exceptional sailor and seemed to have an extra sense of what the sea would do. With Kallisti's tuition, Balor learned that force alone will not always work and that his most vital asset was not his size and strength but his brain intelligently channelling his power. His main trading areas were well outside the Pillars of Hercules and reached up to where the sea turned to ice, and the sun never rose high in the sky. When he travelled south, he turned back when the midday sun was directly overhead. He met so many new peoples, and most were keen to do good business with him.

Balor continued his building skills. He had designed and built the tall Sardinian lookout tower, the Nuralgi, that dominated the port skyline. He made it with his own money. He wanted to give something back to his surrogate home. As the years passed, he and Kallisti grew rich, and he even started to be respected in Sardinia. He had sold the three original Greek ships and had the three great black ships built; they became his distinctive trademark.

Trading for the Sherden had become increasingly difficult for the last few years for two reasons. The first was the sheer number of new trading nations, each building its ships, and the extra ships were all competing on price. The second reason was much harder to deal with. Most of the new settlements in and around the north of the Mediterranean were controlled by the Hittites or the Greeks, and they wanted to benefit exclusively from any trade by using their ships. A similar situation was happening with the southern coast of the Mediterranean; only it was the Egyptians who were in control. The Egyptians did not have trading ships, but they used the Phoenicians.

The Sherden found that they had to change, and they started to hire their services as mercenaries. The Egyptians had no sea warriors, but they now hired mercenaries to fight for them at sea and paid exceptionally well.

Balor went with the rest of the Sherden to help catch the riverboats that had been stolen from the River Nile and taken out to sea. These boats were not fit or safe on the sea, but the culprits had stolen valuables from Egypt, and they had to be captured and returned to Egypt for punishment. Remembering his past, he felt terrible about this task, but all of the Sherden were there, and the money was good, so he reluctantly sailed with the rest.

Small riverboats are notoriously hard to find at sea as they are mostly hidden between the waves. The higher off the waterline the ship's lookout is, the easier the small boats are to find. On this occasion, Balor's three tall ships found the small flotilla of stolen boats in their search area. Balor did not take too long to surround the small riverboats and capture the miscreants. Something did not seem right; these were not just petty thieves.

He let their spokesman on board when he pleaded to talk with him.

"Why do you stop us? We are only trying to save our lives. We used to believe that Egypt was our home forever and for our descendants, but now everything is changing. We are not all master builders and are now not allowed to live in our homes anymore. We are being told to either fight for Egypt in their wars, to take over other countries, or die by their hands for refusing."

Balor looked down at the many small boats swamped by the sea waves. They were packed with men, women, and children, all desperately bailing out water with their hands. They were far too many people for those small boats on a river, but on the sea, they would undoubtedly sink and soon!

Balor then made what was perhaps the most honourable 'big' decision he had ever made in his life. A decision, which would undoubtedly close another country to him, but after all had happened, he was still a Scythian at heart and still had some principles. He could not just blend in and do what his peers would have done in less than a heartbeat.

He loaded all of the fugitives onto his three ships. Then he made sure that every stolen Egyptian boat was capsized. He then sailed north before anyone, even the Sherden, saw what had happened. When he reached Cyprus, he chose a deserted cove and released his precious human cargo to liberty and a new life. They had not stolen valuables and had nothing to give him but their meagre provisions. In gratitude, they offered them to him for saving them from certain death. The offer touched Balor. Instead of accepting their precious food, he gave them more of his supplies; to give them a better chance of surviving in their new land. There would be no money from Egypt for him now, nor would he go there again looking for mercenary work.

Kallisti was annoyed at the lack of money but proud that his protégé indeed did have a Scythian heart. But it still left the problem – where would they get their next cash from?

The World is About to Change.

Ladra, after he had left Partholon in Troy, stopped in Santorini to join up with Antonio. He quickly disembarked, leaving his ship to rejoin the rest of the fleet. The rest of the fleet did not stop as they were making fast progress, and while the conditions were good, they wanted to keep going. Ladra would travel with Antonio to Sardinia to meet up again with the main fleet and his ship. Lightly laden, Antonio's vessel would quickly catch up with the main fleet in Mediterranean waters.

Antonio had made a very profitable exchange of his cargo of Ériu's copper ore, and he promptly exchanged much credit on buying finished Santorinian products. Finished Copper items and exquisite pottery were top of the list, and all were headed for Ériu's best tables. Not excessively expensive, but suitable for important entertaining. Most, of course, would be for Cessair, for her official business, but he had also picked a few choice items for his Banba.

Antonio was noticeably excited when he met Ladra as his boat docked. His welcoming words were.

"The world is about to change! Come with me. You must see this."

He grabbed Ladra by the arm and started heading towards a building not far from the port. The building was not exceptionally large, but it could still securely store a boatload of produce. Part of the building could be used for living, and it was apparent that Antonio had been staying there. With a broad smile on his face, he proudly said.

"This is ours – this is our base in Santorini. I paid for it with some of the value from our sale; we were almost given it; it was such a good exchange."

Ladra was impressed enough with the building and thought it would be beneficial for trading with the Santorinians. Still, Antonio was not so excited over a not-so-spectacular building. There was something else that Antonio was holding back, so Ladra asked straight out.

"The last time I saw you so excited, you had just 'hooked up' with Banba. Don't tell me your mood is so good because of this hut?"

"No! Of course not. Come over to this table and watch."

On the table were two parallel pieces of wood spaced about a foot of distance apart. Laid on top and across the pieces of wood were two thin sheets of what Ladra knew as copper; one was a lighter colour than the other. Antonio picked up a blunt axe and handed it to Ladra. He said.

"Now hit the lighter-coloured sheet with the axe."

Ladra struck a gentle blow on the lighter sheet as he was bid, and the metal sheet did precisely what he expected. It buckled under the axe and folded down to the tabletop. Ladra did not see the point of bending a valuable piece of copper. He even felt guilty for damaging the craftsman's work, so he picked that sheet up and straightened it back, as well as he could, with his bare hands. He scolded Antonio for asking him to cause such evident damage.

Antonio handed him the axe again and then told him to do the same with the darker sheet. A reluctant Ladra again did as he was bid, and he hit the darker sheet with the heavy axe.

Much to Ladra's surprise, the sheet did not buckle, but the axe just bounced off. He looked at the sheet, and it was unmarked. Ladra could not believe what had happened – nothing could be that strong. He started to think that he had missed the centre of the sheet with the axe head. He swung the axe again and hit the sheet extremely hard this time. The sheet did bend, but only very slightly. On the other hand, the axe did not fare so well, as the head flew off the handle it had been attached to.

84

The World is About to Change.

"Incredible."

Was all that Ladra could say as he picked up the sheet to examine it. No matter how hard he tried. He could not bend the sheet with his hands.

"Imagine what can be made with this much stronger material. We could make better spears, axes, knives, or stronger impenetrable armour – our world will change completely."

Now Ladra could see why Antonio was so excited, and he then realised that so was he.

This new material was top secret; Antonio only learned about it because his brother worked where they were making it. It was from him that Antonio had received the sample; what was crucial was that he told them how to make it and what materials were needed. Antonio said.

"This darker sheet is still mostly copper, but they have added some tin when making it. They are calling it Bronze. We need to keep this piece secret and take it to Fintan. We must not get my family into trouble."

A short while later, they were again on Antonio's boat and heading west for Sardinia.

Balor was greeted at the door of Kallisti's house by a familiar face. The little girl jumped up into his arms and shouted.

"Daddy! You are back."

"Ethniu, you have grown. Are you helping grandad again?"

"Yes. He has been terribly upset recently. He has been like this since two men from Ériu told him some awfully bad news. He speaks

to very few people now and sits alone in his room or the garden. He is there now, under the big tree as usual.".

Balor could easily guess what news had been told to his partner and wife's father. He also knew that his meeting would be exceedingly difficult in the next few seconds. He turned to his daughter and said.

"Run home. Tell your mother that I will be back soon. I need to talk to your grandfather alone."

The anger had left Kallisti and was replaced by an empty, hollow feeling. He looked at Balor with a sadness in his eye that was new. His first words were spoken in a calm and matter-of-fact tone.

"You will have to take your family and leave Sardinia."

Balor was devastated. Of all possible punishments, this was by far the worst. He had made his life here; his home was here, and he had hoped it would have his future here also. Kallisti continued even though it was difficult for him.

"I pleaded for you at the council, and there was almost unanimous agreement that you had helped our country greatly. But everyone agreed that Sardinia could not be seen as the permanent home of someone who attacks ships at sea outside of a war. Sardinia cannot protect you from the Hittites seeking vengeance; we cannot have them come here to capture you. Nor can we afford to lose the Hittite ships stopping here for supplies, either.

You are not banned from here – you cannot live here permanently."

Balor was lost for words. His world was about to change again. His following words were not entirely selfish, even though they only contained the pronoun 'I.'

The World is About to Change.

"Where will I go? What will I do?

Balor had not forgotten his family or his crews. He saw them as extensions of himself, a form of the royal 'we.'

The next few hours were spent considering Balor's options. There seemed to be very few of them left. Trading would now be difficult as news of the raid on the Hittite boat had already circulated the Mediterranean. Nowhere there can act as his home. They, too, would have the same problems as Sardinia would. It was Kallisti that concluded that his options were minimal. He said.

"If you must continue your business on the sea, you must find a home outside the Pillars of Hercules. Somewhere where your enemies will not follow you."

Balor then remembered a place he had visited once a few years earlier. He reminded Kallisti about it with the words.

"Remember the time that I went to collect axes from Angus? I was returning home by going the long way around Ériu. Just as I had crossed the north of that country and started to head south, the sea turned very rough, and I had to seek shelter urgently. I lost my sense of direction and thought we would surely drown. Just before me, I saw this island; it was so close that we almost ran aground. Well, then, I found a true haven; a well-protected and sheltered harbour. That island saved our lives.

I will go there!"

"Perfect!"

Replied Kallisti, and then he continued.

"I can't blame you for taking what was not theirs from the Hittites. If I were much younger, I might have done the same thing;

they need to be taught a lesson. Unfortunately, the world is changing, and so are its values."

Balor felt better that his friend and mentor had not lost faith in him completely. He also felt better in that he could see a way forward for himself, his crew, and his family – in that order. Almost as an afterthought, he asked.

"Would you please look after Ethniu? That is until we become established in our new remote island."

For the first time in weeks, the old man smiled and replied.

"Of course! She is always welcome here. She will be great company for me.

Load plenty of supplies. Now hurry, winter is coming fast, and the seas there will soon be too rough.

Many Ériu's ships carrying new settlers will stop here soon; be gone before they come."

A couple of days later, three black ships left the port carrying Balor, his crews, and Cethlenn.

Antonio and Ladra arrived in Sardinia to rejoin the main fleet. The fleet was already resupplied, and everyone was eager to move on the following dawn.

Ladra and Antonio had to see Kallisti, even if only for a brief visit. The old man had been shocked by the news they had given him not that many weeks earlier. They were worried about him.

Ethniu welcomed the two and brought them to see her grandfather. As she walked, she said.

"Grandfather is much happier now."

The World is About to Change.

Kallisti was in a much better mood, and his characteristic smile had returned. They discussed the changing settlements around the Mediterranean and how trading changed how countries viewed each other.

In the past, countries like Affreidg just got on with life. They produced what they could, and most improvements came from within. News from different countries was exceedingly rare and often months, but usually years, out of date. Travellers from other countries were even more infrequent. Kallisti then said.

"Every day, a boat arrives in our port from another country. They carry the latest news that is only a few days old. By the end of the week, we know most of the information from around the Mediterranean, and the news from beyond is only a few weeks old!

Take the news of Balor's taking those goods from the Hittite boat. Every single ship that enters this port knows about it. Some condemn it outright, saying that; 'no boat, which is not at war, should attack another,' often adding 'the sea is dangerous enough without people attacking others.' There are, however, a great many people, and I am one of them, who say that 'the Hittites exploiting the new settlers was the real crime, and they deserved what they got!'"

Ladra and Antonio listened carefully to the old man's words. They had sympathy for both sides of the argument and could not decide which side was worse, for there was little dignity on either side.

Kallisti then told them how Balor saved the refugees from Egypt despite the cost to him by angering a mighty nation. Antonio was surprised and suggested that he must have had some ulterior motive. Ladra was quick to defend Balor with the words.

"That is much more like the behaviour of Balor as a boy; the Balor that I knew; he was not all bad!"

Kallisti was also quick to reply.

"I am glad that you said that! Balor is moving his home to an island close to Ériu!"

Kallisti waited for the news to sink in before he changed the emphasis by saying.

"Balor and his kind are not the real developing blight in the world. The problem we are facing is that powerful countries are now trying to dominate and exploit other newer or smaller countries. The Egyptians and the Hittites are racing to see who can control most of the Mediterranean coast; the Greeks have joined that race! Without this globalisation and exploitive practice, there would be no Balor or his kind."

It was now exceptionally late, and even though the arguments were becoming involved and hotly debated, it was time for Ladra and Antonio to go. They reluctantly said goodbye to their hosts, Kallisti and Ethniu. As they walked back down to their boats that night, they commented on the kindness, hospitality, and what a lovely, well-mannered girl Ethniu was; they still had no idea who her father was.

Bith and Bairrfhind had made quick progress to Wexford. The route was regularly travelled, easy-going, and well-marked. From there, they chose a way that was always close to the sea. They spent much of the trip following the long beaches, and the progress then was quick and easy. When the coast became challenging to follow because of cliffs or other obstacles, they moved inland into the dense broadleaf woodland.

The World is About to Change.

It was often hard to see the sea as much of their route north was covered by trees. This woodland had little undergrowth except where a large tree had recently fallen, and even there, many wild herbivores, such as boars, kept a vast network of paths open and passable.

As they moved north, they saw a ridge of mountains inland of them, coming closer and closer to their route by the sea. They were tired of travelling under the canopy, seeing no further ahead than a few trees, so they decided to move a few kilometres inland and climb the mountains. As they climbed, the trees first thinned and then disappeared altogether. The view from the mountain ridge was spectacular.

To the west was the coast of Ériu, with the shaggy carpet of green trees dominating all the lands between the mountains and the sea. The tree cover extended south as far as their eyes could see. Far out to sea, they saw the land of the sister island they had passed when they first arrived. Seeing such a large expanse of land with no evidence of any man having been there before was a strange feeling. It made their small group feel isolated and vulnerable. Bairrfhind spoke first; her keen young eyes had seen something relevant to the moment.

"Look there! Far to the south! That is where we came from, Wexford. Do you see the smoke from the signalling fire? Or it could be a fire clearing some forest there."

Bith didn't, but that didn't matter; they were not isolated and alone. They continued north along the ridge of mountains. The paths now, across the mountain tops, were laid more by rabbits and deer. A little later, Bairrfhind had seen something else, far out to sea.

"There are three ships sailing north a long way out to sea. They are not Ladra's that far out. I wonder if they are Phoenician traders going to visit Angus."

When they reached the end of the ridge of mountains, they made a temporary camp as they planned their route. The view earlier had been dominated by trees and seas. Impressive as it was, it was unimpressive compared to the view ahead of them. Ahead of them was everything that a settler could want. Bith was excited and spoke first.

"Look at those rivers! That flat fertile land. All that grass. See those huge flocks of birds? There must be thousands and thousands of them. We must tell Cessair about this and suggest that she create a new settlement here; it is a perfect place. See that big black pool where that little river joins the big river; it would safely moor Ladra's entire fleet. We must call this place 'Black pool' or 'Dublin.'"

One of the rivers looked quite large and challenging to cross close to the coast so they would move several kilometres inland.

Crossing the grassland was easy enough, but the river required the making of several boats. Everything they needed was close to hand, and again this confirmed to Bith that a settlement should be established there soon.

Grassland interspersed with woodland dominated the travelling for the next few days.

"All great land for our crops."

Said Bith to his wife as they made their way further north. The land for miles around was flat, and when the forest again started to dominate the landscape, they had few landmarks to show them the way. They knew, however, that moss grew much better on the northern side of the tree. On the other hand, Ivy grew more vigorously on the southern side with smaller, denser, pointier leaves.

They continued until the land fell away, down the sides of a winding river valley. They were looking for a place to cross the river without much effort when Bairrfhind spoke.

The World is About to Change.

"Look! There! I saw someone, a woman, I think. She saw us and ran away. She went that way, upriver."

This was big news for the travelling group, and everyone started running. They chased the girl from their side of the river. The girl was scared and was shouting out for help as she ran. None of Bith's group wanted to scare the unknown girl but having not seen any other humans for several weeks, they could not contain their excitement. The girl had disappeared into a belt of trees but could not be far away.

Bith's party was in great form. They had travelled up through Ériu and were now approaching their destination. Everyone was enthusiastically scrambling to be the first to make proper contact with the clan in Sí an Bhrú. They all wanted to cross the river, but each place they tried was too deep to wade across.

On the other side, amongst the trees, was a group of people gathering in the dense woodland. This must be their destination, but why were the people holding back under cover of the dense foliage?

Finally, Bith's party found a shallower point to cross the river, and they started to wade into the water.

They were up to their waists in water when the first warning arrow hit the water close to Bith.

Bith shouted out.

"That is no way to show hospitality to weary travellers!"

Within seconds, the far bank was swarming with people offering help and apologising profusely. The girl had called for help, and the tribe had responded without further thinking.

Attacking any human being was against their laws, but to shoot an arrow first was a fundamental breach of the rules. To fire an arrow at the father of Ériu's leader and his wife, a very senior Brehon, was irredeemable. The Brehons would need to be called. Bairrfhind herself would be at the centre of a significant decision regarding what should be done with the person who fired the arrow.

Bith and Bairrfhind were glad to have reached Sí an Bhrú. They could rest there for the winter. They were tired after their long and arduous journey. It was hardly the welcoming committee they expected, but the unfortunate arrow incident was soon forgotten as everyone crowded around to hear about their discoveries en route.

Balor Finds a New Home.

The three black ships made good progress as they travelled west through the Pillars of Hercules. The route north was also plain sailing. Balor had travelled this way many times in the last few years, and he was becoming more confident crossing the broader stretches of the sea, which meant leaving the safety of the coast behind.

He was starting to read the sea and the sky quite well, and he was now competent at forecasting the sea conditions a few hours ahead. He passed Angus' Island without stopping. He was keen to set up his new island home before the winter storms started to set in. But once they rounded the north of Ériu, the seas became rougher and harder to navigate.

The island they almost bumped into the last time was not to be found easily. The rough sea made it extremely hard to see anywhere some distance ahead of them. They could see the land to their left, a kilometre or so away; the island should be somewhere on their right.

The night would soon be upon them, and they needed to find land and shelter before dark. Balor wished there was a fire on the island to guide them and give them hope for a warm, safe, and easy landing. He remembered the comforting feeling he had each time he approached and saw the signal firelight emanating from his old hometown in Sardinia. He had seen Ériu's beacon fires at each settlement they had passed. But there was no light around him to be seen that evening.

Balor was about to head for the mainland to find a safely sheltered cove when a keen-eyed young sailor shouted.

"An island ahead and on our right."

The island loomed up quickly, and Balor hurriedly headed for one of the sheltered coves on the leeward side. He remembered the cove very well. It was well sheltered from most winds other than those coming from a south, south easterly direction. It had a sandy bottom and a smooth sandy beach; it was ideal for landing upon.

When he entered the cove at speed, the sheltered sea was now calm, but dead ahead, there was no sandy beach to be seen. Just where he had planned to beach his boats, it now looked just like a field of large and dangerous boulders, any one of which could damage his boats, especially if they were hit at speed.

There was panic as the crews tried to slow the boats before the pending collision. Some ran to throw out anchors, but there was no time, and everyone braced themselves for what was about to happen. This was not the way that Balor wanted to arrive at his new home.

The boat was only metres away when the 'boulders' parted and fled into the sea. There had been so many grey seals that no grain of sand could be seen; Balor's ships had disturbed a huge sleeping colony. A few minutes later, the beach was deserted save for three safely beached boats. The cove waters, however, were now 'alive' with disgruntled seals, which did not like the intrusion of the new company.

Balor's new home was about five kilometres from the western tip to the east and only one kilometre at its widest. It was surrounded by tall vertical cliffs constantly beaten by the wild Atlantic waves. The few small, sheltered coves were lined by tall cliff faces, which were impossible to climb, leaving the beach as the only practical entry point. The island was a natural fortress and ideal for Balor and his people.

There was a grand celebration that night, but they all knew they had much work to achieve before winter set in properly. It was cold that first night, but nobody noticed. The following day, work did start in earnest.

There was some timber on the island, but it could have been of better quality and quantity. It was good enough to build houses, but by far, the best building resource was flat stone of all sizes. Balor did not take long to have the first few buildings built and roofed with these ideal stones. There was land that could grow crops, but Balor's strategy differed from most normal settlers.

Balor had realised that warfare on land was predictable. The largest army usually won. The next influence was technology. Troops with newer, more efficient equipment carried more weight. A single charioteer could scythe through a dozen men on foot if they were armed only with short spears. If the two sides were well balanced, strategy came into play, but until now, it had yet to make a significant difference.

He realised that he would have to face an enemy that would want to stop him sooner or later. He had to change how these battles were fought so that he could alter the odds in his favour. He had realised early on that all battles had taken place on land. There had been centuries to develop strategies to defeat small groups on the ground, and he knew that any small group pursued by a powerful nation was doomed to failure from the start. The weakest element of any group's defence was always their homes and family.

A big nation's attack strategy against small groups was a 'Scorched Earth policy.' They would attack their enemies' homes, kill their families, including their children, and destroy their crops and animals. Any enemy combatants left alive had nothing to live on or to fight for as their 'world', in all senses, had been destroyed and laid waste. Balor did not want this to happen to his people.

Balor's ships were strong, agile, and capable of holding their own against any other ship in the known world. So, he had the technological advantage. Any nation likely to come after him did not have warships, and they relied instead on trading ships, most of whom he already knew and was friendly with. Most traders in their world based their trade on trust. Sure, they tried to make the most profitable deals possible, but the trading code banned blatant exploitation. There was great resentment amongst the traders against the 'big' nations that exploited settlements and backed them up with threats and force. These traders secretly hailed Balor as a folk hero.

Cethlenn was pleased with the stone house that Balor had built for them. It was equipped with the best of the known world's luxuries. Unlike many of the women there, Cethlenn liked to stay in and around the home and on dry land. She asked Balor.

"Will we be safe here?"

"Knowledge is power."

Replied Balor.

"If anyone wants to attack, I have the advantage. I am safe on my inaccessible island, and they will be all at sea. I can fight them when or if it suits me, not them. I know these seas better than anyone, which is another advantage I have; at sea, I can lead them to my choice of the battle site.

This island of mine will become my fortress. I can quickly destroy any ships trying to land using weapons from the flanking cliffs. That is, if they ever find this place. They can never lay siege to this place as the sea is rarely calm for that long. I will make this place a new haven for anyone who thinks like us."

Cethlenn then asked.

"What about the people of Ériu? Are you going to see them? Like you, they are Scythian also.

Balor thought for a while, and then he said.

"I will visit a local colony before winter and try to become friends with them. It may be difficult, though."

Cethlenn then added the words.

"Bring plenty of gifts; everybody likes gifts."

A few days later, Balor loaded two ships with gifts and other exotic goods and headed for Broadhaven. As he left his island behind, he noticed how rapidly he lost sight of it and how quickly it visually merged into the sea and sky. He made a mental note that he had to make a Nuralgi. He would surround his tower with reflective metal so it could be seen from many miles away. This Sardinian-inspired guide tower would lead him to safety under challenging conditions. Furthermore, the tower platform would give a lookout early warning of approaching ships. Yes, he, the master builder, would start his masterpiece this winter.

A group of small children were playing by the signal fire that overlooked the Broadhaven Stags. They had heard the story of how their leader had seen the spirit of Ériu there, and now the place had become a favourite place for children to visit and to look for Ancients. They knew that the Ancients revealed themselves to only a few special people, and they all hoped they were special. They sang and danced, calling out for the Ancients to visit them; this was a great game but also a little scary!

A small boy saw a black speck in the sea. At first, he had hardly noticed it, but it had caught his attention, and his mind was primed and ready to imagine anything. The next time he looked, it appeared no closer, but now it was large and menacing. It looked as though two black ancients had arisen from the ocean's depths to come and claim him as their own. He screamed at the top of his voice.

*"**Fomorians!** They came from out of the sea. They are coming for us. Fomorians, Fomorians are coming; **run!**"*

Fear spread rapidly throughout the group of children, and they all fled to the safety of their homes and families. They had a long way to run but never slowed until they returned home safely. They were breathless and terrified, and the tribe adults were also concerned about what had happened to these ordinarily sensible children. All that their children would say and repeat over and over was.

"Fomorians, Fomorians, Fomorians are coming!"

What was coming from under the sea to scare this group? The adults were all discussing this, trying to understand what had upset them so dramatically. Just then, two large and menacing black ships sailed straight into Broadhaven.

These were the first ever visiting ships, and they were still determining what to do. The Brehon rules were clear on the subject, but visitors had never come to Broadhaven before. The senior Brehon was consulted, and his reply was swift and precise.

"We give shelter and, if necessary, sanctity to all travellers."

Some were doubtful as the ships looked very menacing, but the Brehons were to be obeyed in matters of law. The first ship docked, and the second moored alongside the first. The Brehon was pushed to the front to welcome the travellers.

It did not take long for Balor to work out that the man designated to welcome him was not the local tribe leader, but he would treat him as though he were. Balor spoke first.

"I come in peace."

The Brehon and everyone else in that welcoming committee visibly lightened up and became more relaxed. The reply was now given with confidence.

"Come, traveller. You are welcome to Broadhaven. How may we help you? Have you come far?"

Balor and his crew were invited on land, and they were taken to a place where they could talk. It was Balor who did most of the talking, and in many ways, he led the meeting.

He explained how he had moved to an island a few hours north of Broadhaven. He and his people were traders, but they disagreed with the trading behaviour of the big-bullying countries. As he said those words, he remembered that he had been considered a bully when he lived in Affreidg. He now understood, perhaps for the first time, why his former Scythian people had resented his bullying.

Nevertheless, now was the time to put the past in the past and forge new alliances with his former compatriots.

"These gifts are for you here in Broadhaven. They are spices and herbs from distant lands and many other rare items from lands that are far, far away."

Balor then sent some of his men to bring the gifts ashore. There was great excitement all around, and the news spread rapidly throughout the local settlements. There was a feast rapidly organised, and Balor and his crew were to be the guests of honour. People came from around, and there was a joyous and happy atmosphere.

The young children had recovered from their earlier shock and watched the black ships while they remained hidden behind some large rocks. They watched as the black ship's crews left for the party that was called in their honour. They were mesmerised; they had never seen people like them before. One whispered.

"Look! That man has a stick for a leg. That one has only one arm."

Another said.

"Look at the colour of that man. He is as black as their boat and as large as two normal people."

"And that man is tiny and almost yellow! And he has only one eye! Maybe these are Fomorians?

Before running home to hide in his bed, the third child hardly finished his words. He was just as scared as before; he was sure that these were creatures from under the sea that had arrived, and the other kids just laughed at their friend.

The party was a rip-roaring success; everyone agreed that Balor and his people were welcome anytime. Many romantic relationships were also started at that party, and they must be given a chance to blossom. The stories of the travellers' adventures and encounters kept the locals enthralled and eager to hear more from their superstar visitors.

The following day, the celebrities boarded their ships laden with fresh local produce, ready to travel back to their island. Balor re-emerged from his boat carrying a beautifully crafted sealed box. He gave it to the Brehon leader with the words.

"This is a personal gift for Cessair. Please give it to her. We grew up together, and we parted on bad terms. Please tell her I am sorry and would like to make amends."

The number of kids hidden behind the rocks this morning had grown considerably. They had come to see the spectacle of these odd-looking people for themselves.

The kids started chanting when the black ships travelled safely from Broadhaven.

"Fomorians, Fomorians, Fomorians.

There go the Fomorians!"

Fini Volume 4.

Postscript.

Postscript.

The Copper Age includes a period when there was a massive movement of peoples moving west from the Near East. I postulate in this series of books that this movement was precipitated by the flooding of the area now known as the Black Sea. While my hypothesis may be new, the vast movement of peoples flooding Europe is, and has been, well-accepted by historians for many centuries. This period merges into the Bronze Age, with the knowledge and ability to enhance the properties of copper by adding tin. This period was associated closely with the development of international sea trading.

These historians also well-accepted the rise of Phoenician trading throughout the Mediterranean area. Inherent to the process of third-party trading is the concept of profit. Until widespread international trading, the traditional method of swapping one type of goods for another was based on equitable bargains or trust of a fair bargain being made by the end of the transaction, sometimes days, months, or years later.

This period of a dramatic increase in social and economic intercourse brought with it the problems associated with the prospect of creating wealth without actually producing goods. This added value concept as a 'legitimate' business interest gave rise to and encouraged other less well-accepted practices of creating wealth without making things, practices such as theft or piracy.

Many countries that were to become the superpowers of the late Bronze Age developed their trade protection on land only. They failed to see the importance of developing an effective naval defence; instead, they relied on the logistical trading support of the Phoenicians.

The sea areas remained the effective Wild West of a much later period but of more familiar American fame. This continued until most Mediterranean maritime cities were destroyed at the end of the Bronze Age, c.1200 BCE. At that late stage, the true importance of sea supremacy became blatantly obvious.

The Fomorians have usually been treated or interpreted as mythical monsters. Their shape and form vary from disconcerting, as in disfigured, missing limbs or senses, to fantastical, otherworldly, and indescribable. Even the much later church-influenced transcribed chronicles are very circumspect about their origins. But most references acknowledge that the Fomorians and the Tuathe de Danann originated from the same people and that they recognised each other as kin.

Balor has left many marks on the Irish psyche, both psychologically and physically. Phrases such as giving 'The evil Eye' are sometimes uttered as 'Balor's Eye' or naming an island, off the coast of Donegal, as Tory Island. Tory (Tower Island) after his Nuralgi and the tower site on that island as Balor's fort!

At their peak, the Fomorians held dominion over a vast area of western coastal regions between the west of Ireland and the Baltic countries.

As the centuries passed, the various sea peoples established permanent land-based communities. The Fomorians settled around the Balkan Sea, and then in later centuries, they morphed into the Vikings.

This series of books has been written to offer an alternative history of Ireland. A story about the little island in the Atlantic Ocean that has influenced and benefitted the world.

These books are written, for a broad audience, in a readable story format. They introduce Cessair, the original settler who worked with nature, Partholon an exploiting businessman, Phoenician sea traders, Fomorian sea pirates, The FirBolg or Bag Men, The Tuathe de Danann, the Druids or magic people and the Milesians, the descendants of Scotia the daughter of an Egyptian Pharoah, plus many others.

These books have been written to inspire an interest in investigating what really happened to the people on the island of Ireland since the Ice Age. The author has drawn evidence from ancient texts and associated commentaries. He has added the latest scientific findings and analysis to construct a possible and plausible history that is free of political bias.

Successive conquering invaders have written Ireland's popular history for many centuries. It has been reported to glorify and justify why those invaders invaded the island rather than face many uncomfortable truths. For example, the victors annulled women's equal status and power; this had been enshrined in Irish Brehon law from the earliest of times.

The series starts with flooding a vast area of highly fertile land 7600 years ago; this area is now known as 'The Black Sea.' It follows the stories of characters named in the ancient Irish texts that changed Ireland. It describes how the farming and metalworking Irish stood well apart from the rest of the hunter-gathers in Northern Europe and how, instead, they had close ties with the Eastern Mediterranean and Egypt via the then highly active sea routes.

The series covers the collapse of the Mediterranean civilisation at the end of the Bronze Age. Later volumes show how Ireland led the Isles of Britain to be the first area in the world to declare itself Christian in AD 250, well before Rome and centuries before St Patrick arrived.